Kiss Midnight Goodbye

Kiss Midnight Goodbye

Midnight Blue Beach
Book Three

By

Olivia Jaymes

www.OliviaJaymes.com

KISS MIDNIGHT GOODBYE

Kiss Midnight Goodbye

Secrets revealed…

Peyton Nelson travels to London to find the truth about her irresponsible late-husband and all of the lies he's told through the years. Without a doubt, her family knows more than they've let on.

Dizzying passion…

Detective Ellis Hunter is a man on a mission. He'll keep Peyton safe from the people who want to kill her no matter what it costs him. But the true danger is how they're beginning to feel about one another. He might save her life but lose his heart.

Painful truth…

It's the two of them against the powerful and secretive Evandria organization and only one side will be victorious. The lines between good and evil are blurred and Peyton and Ellis only know one thing for sure…trust no one but each other.

Chapter One

PEYTON NELSON LINKED her arm through Ellis's and led him through Notting Hill to her brother's flat. It had been over a year since she'd visited Jensen but the charming neighborhood hadn't changed much. The funky art gallery was still on the corner and that little bookstore she'd stumbled into when it was pouring rain was across the street.

"He knows we're coming?" Ellis asked, his entire body tense as his gaze swept back and forth from one side of the street to the other. Detective Ellis Hunter was charged with keeping Peyton safe and he took that responsibility quite seriously.

"I called him when we checked into the hotel," Peyton assured him. "He's thrilled to see his baby sister."

"Me? He'd rather I wasn't around."

Peyton rolled her eyes at Ellis's sardonic tone. "Hardly. As much as he and I love each other, we've never inserted ourselves into each other's lives. I see him at the holidays and that's about it. He'll probably pour you a drink and drive you crazy with questions about being a cop in America. He watches too much television so he's going to think you're just like the detectives in his favorite shows."

"How much does he know?"

Good question. She'd been wondering that very thing the entire flight from Virginia to London. "I'm not sure. He knows that I was in an explosion and was in a coma. He knows I have questions about Evandria and Greg because that's what I said to him when I called. But I do know he's a member and that means he might know a hell of a lot more than we do. So for now, I'm planning to try and get him to tell me all that he knows."

Ellis's lips twisted into a half smile. "Give me fifteen minutes with him and he'll tell us everything he knows and all his secrets."

Elbowing him hard in the ribs, she gave him her best disgusted look. "You will not interrogate my brother like one of your street perps. We will discuss this calmly and rationally like the adults we are." She grinned gleefully. "Besides, I can always tell when he's lying."

"Because you're psychic."

Another dig in the ribs. Harder this time. "I am not psychic. I said I believe in psychics although they're rare. No, Jensen is just a terrible liar. He has tells."

Ellis smiled as they rounded the corner. "You have a tell too, princess. You rub the back of your ear when you are being less than truthful."

"Less than truthful," she echoed. "You mean lying. Just say it."

"Fine. When you lie you rub the back of your ear."

Stopping in the middle of the sidewalk, she ignored the funny looks they were attracting from passersby. If there was one thing she'd learned in her life it was to ignore what strangers thought. It was hard enough to please yourself and maybe a few family or friends.

"When have I ever lied to you?"

It was his turn to roll his eyes. "Are you kidding? Peyton, you should lie down and rest. *I'm not tired, Ellis*. When you clearly are. Peyton, you should take your pain meds. *My head doesn't hurt, Ellis*. When it clearly does. Should I go on?"

No, he shouldn't. She got it.

"I just don't like people fussing over me and frankly, by the time I woke up I was already sick and tired of being in the hospital and on those pain pills. They made my thinking fuzzy."

"I know—that's why I never said anything."

Ellis wasn't an eloquent man. He'd described himself to her as a simple, direct individual who tried to do right more often than not but often found himself tired, grouchy, and frustrated with people and bureaucracy.

He was all those things but he was also kind and giving, always putting her wants and needs before his own. Her comfort and safety was far more important than anything he wanted. Being treated so special…it was a first for her. While she couldn't help but love being cared for so diligently, it also made her a little uncomfortable. As if she didn't deserve it.

She tried to remember instances when her late husband Greg had put her first but one didn't come immediately to mind. He was sure to have of course, but the fact that she couldn't think of any off the top of her head said a lot.

Most of it about her. She'd gotten married too young and then stayed that way for all the wrong reasons. Now look where she was. Questioning her brother about a secret society that had murdered her husband and his two friends along with others, she was sure.

"There it is." Peyton pointed to a row of homes. "His is the light blue one with the black door."

"It's very…British," observed Ellis with a grin. "Although to be honest I don't know a damn thing about the UK except that I like their television shows."

Anyone overhearing the conversation would think he was talking about Dr. Who and Sherlock. He did love those shows but he also avidly watched "The Great British Baking Show".

Peyton checked her watch. "He should be home from work by now."

"What does he do again?"

She'd told Ellis before but she had the feeling he didn't quite believe it.

"He's a banker of sorts. International finance and trade."

They stopped at the bottom of the steps. "Translation?"

"He puts together deals for international corporations. Helps them secure financing."

Ellis shoved his hands in the pockets of his trousers. "Sounds boring as hell."

"It is," Peyton confirmed. "That's why he'll be asking you about your job. Much more exciting."

"If you like paperwork and bad coffee."

Jensen must have been watching out of the windows for them because the front door swung open and he stood there with his arms open, waiting for his hug. She ran into his arms and he squeezed her tightly, his hand running over her head.

"Thank God your head is as hard as it is."

Her brother was the funny one in the family. "Ha ha, so cute. Next time you can spend several days in a coma and wake up with doctors asking you who the president is."

Jensen chuckled and ushered them inside. "I'm just happy that you're okay. You are all healed, right? No lasting effects?"

"Right as rain." Peyton linked her arm with Ellis's again, pulling him closer. "Ellis, this is my brother Jensen. Jensen, this is Detective Ellis Hunter."

The two men shook hands, clearly sizing each other up, but seemed mostly satisfied with what they saw. There aggressive stances relaxed and their body language loosened up.

Good, no pissing contest.

She was struck by the differences in the two men as they stood facing each other. Where Jensen was blond and fair, Ellis was dark-haired with golden skin from the sun. Her brother was tall and lean, and had been described as gangly in his youth. Ellis, on the other hand, while only an inch or two shorter was powerfully built, not the kind of man you'd want to tangle with in a dark alley.

"It's nice to meet you," Jensen said, walking over to a bar in the corner. "Can I get you a drink?"

Ellis held up his hand. "I'm good. Peyton?"

She shook her head. After that long flight from the States, her head was pounding. She was going to need to take a pain pill when they got back to the hotel.

"Not for me."

Jensen indicated a beige leather sofa as he settled into a matching chair next to it. "Then have a seat. You wanted to talk to me about Evandria."

This was the moment they'd talked about, planned for but Peyton was finding that it was easier said than done. She was about to ask her brother – in a roundabout way – if he'd known that Greg was murdered. Oh, and had he been part of the conspiracy?

It was going to make Thanksgiving a little tense.

Ellis took pity on her when she hesitated. "We found out Greg was a member of Arsenal."

Jensen frowned. "The football club?"

She had no idea what he was talking about.

"What?"

Leaning forward, he rested his elbows on his knees. "Arsenal, the football club. Us Americans call it soccer. Are you saying that Greg was a member of the team? I find that hard to believe."

"What your sister means is that Greg was a member of the Arsenal division in Evandria," Ellis said smoothly, keeping his expression and tone neutral. He sounded like he was discussing the weather and not a group of people who might be killing their enemies. "Did you know that? Are you also a member?"

"I'm not. I've never actually heard of that division in all the years I've been in Evandria. Are you sure it exists?"

"We're sure," Peyton replied tightly. Boy, were they sure. "So you've never heard of it?"

"No, but I've been pretty concentrated in the financial area. Dad was in that division so I naturally drifted there when I joined."

Ellis leaned forward, his eyes narrowing. "See? That's some-thing I've been wondering about. Peyton knew about Evandria because your father was a member. You're also a member. Greg was a member along with most of your friends I'm guessing. How come Evandria didn't recruit Peyton?"

Jensen's smile widened. "I distinctly remember a conversation between Mom and Dad when I accepted the invitation to join. Mom said that Peyton would join over her dead, cold, stiff body and although Dad blustered and complained she was always going to win."

Peyton wished she had been there for that but as usual she was an outsider in her own family. She'd never been what people might call "close" to her parents. They were almost strangers to her for the most part. "Why do you suppose Mom felt that way?"

Shrugging, Jensen propped his ankle on his opposite knee. "I don't know but she sounded damn sure. I'm guessing she probably wanted to save you from the boring meetings and the endless social commitments. You always hated stuff like that and you wanted to be left alone to do your own thing. I think Mom was just making sure you got to do that. Are you upset that you didn't join? It's not too late."

Not in a million years.

"I think I'll pass." Now for the stickier questions. "What do you know about an internal war in Evandria for control?"

"I've heard stories but never seen anything myself."

Ellis stiffened next to her but she didn't know what had caused him to suddenly tense. Was it Jensen's answer?

Time to stress him a bit. See if he reacted. "Greg was murdered by Evandria."

The color drained from Jensen's face and he opened his

7

mouth to speak but no words came out. Jumping to his feet, he began to pace the small space between the chair and fireplace.

"Evandria wouldn't do that," he finally said, coming to a halt in front of them. "They don't kill people. We're a philanthropic organization trying to make the world a better place."

Ellis placed a hand on hers. "That's what we've heard but we do have proof that certain people in Evandria have, indeed, been killing to grab more power. Arsenal was an initiative started to control that, but clearly it's failed spectacularly. Greg was murdered along with his two friends Alex and Frank, plus Stephen Baxter. They're currently trying to kill Nigel Holmwood and Grant Hollister, although your fearless leader Archer Caldwell has been taken into Evandria custody for triple murder. I doubt he's going to be able to hold onto control of the organization after this."

Jensen's eyes widened and his throat bobbed. He looked like he almost wanted to cry, shaking his head and muttering to himself.

"Alex and Frank too? Their deaths were an accident."

Peyton grabbed on to his words. "You knew them?"

Shrugging, Jensen shuffled his feet. "Sure. I saw them at meetings a few times over the years."

"They were killed just like Greg," Peyton said, not able to keep still. Standing, she walked over to the window and looked out onto the quiet street.

"Greg's death was an accident. He had an allergic reaction."

"Archer Caldwell admitted to paying off the chef at the restaurant to put a large amount of peanut powder into the food."

Jensen sank back down into a chair, his skin pale. "I'm having trouble believing what you're saying."

Ellis glanced at Peyton and she nodded. It was time.

"Maybe this will help you believe it," Ellis said, pulling the cell phone from his pocket and placing it on the table between him and Jensen. He started the recording and the room grew quiet as the sound of Archer's voice filled their ears along with the unknown accomplice. Jensen visibly started when he heard his own name. Shaking his head, he buried his face in his hands with a groan as the recording ended.

Tucking the phone back into his jacket, Ellis cleared his throat. "Do you know who Archer is speaking with?"

Her brother looked up, his eyes watery and bloodshot. "No, I have no idea. They're talking about another Jensen. It's not me."

Peyton wanted to take pity on her brother but they needed answers. If he knew something he needed to say so. "Jensen is an unusual name. It's okay if you know the person. It doesn't mean you knew they were going to kill Greg."

"I don't know," Jensen stated, falling back against the cushions, his arm over his face. "I don't know that voice."

He wouldn't look at her. His expression was hidden by his hand and he was avoiding her direct gaze.

Jensen was lying. He'd done the exact same thing when her parents had questioned him about a party he'd thrown during his senior year in high school while they were out of town. All drama and victimhood, he'd thrown himself on their couch in the exact same position he was sitting in now.

"Are you sure?" she pressed. "Not even a guess? It would help us immensely."

He was still hiding behind his arm. "Not a clue. I wish I could help you."

Placing her hand on Ellis's arm, she squeezed hard when it looked like he was going to question her brother further. There was no point when Jensen was like this. But she remembered that party in high school well. After Jensen had convinced their parents he hadn't thrown that party, he'd been left to stew in his own guilt for a few days. He'd admitted the truth eventually and she hoped this time would end up the same. He had a hell of a lot more to feel guilty about this time, so it might not take too long.

A question flickered over Ellis's features but he didn't question her in front of Jensen.

"I guess we should be going," Peyton said, giving her brother a smile. "You've worked all day and must be tired."

He sat straight up and she could see that his color had returned. "Not yet, you just got here. I can order in some dinner and you can tell me what you've been up to since you left Paris."

Mostly trying to solve the murder of my husband.

"Other than getting blown up?" she joked, trying to keep things light now that she saw Jensen wasn't ready to talk about whatever he knew. He'd definitely lied about knowing something about Arsenal. What she wasn't sure about was whether he'd known about Greg's murder. For now, she was going to give him the benefit of the doubt.

"Other than that," Jensen laughed, standing and heading into the kitchen, rummaging in a drawer before coming back with a stack of takeout menus. "Chinese? Italian? Indian? Pretty much everything you could want is around here. Take your pick."

Ellis reached for the menus and smiled, although it didn't reach his eyes. He didn't trust her brother either. "We appreciate the hospitality."

His entire demeanor brightening, Jensen turned his attention to Ellis. "Maybe over dinner you can tell me some cop stories? I'd love to hear about some of the cases you've worked on."

"I could do that but I warn you now they're not nearly as exciting as on television—but a few are quite weird."

Like this one? Nothing had gone as planned since she'd met her new friends Bailey and Willow. Everything she'd thought she knew about her life and marriage was being called into question. Truth and lies were all mixed up.

One thing was clear. Jensen knew more than he was saying.

Chapter Two

"HE KNEW SOMETHING," Ellis growled into the phone when they returned to their hotel. He was talking to his friend Chase who was back in Williamsburg and updating him on the meeting with Jensen. "I know he does. Peyton assured me that she agrees with me but that he's not ready to fess up to what he knows yet. She told me we need to give him time."

Time they didn't really have. Each moment that they didn't find who had tried to kill Peyton was another moment that she was still in danger. Right now they were relatively safe in their room, Peyton soaking in the tub, but he didn't know how long the peacefulness would last.

"How much time?" Chase asked, frustration in his tone.

"She said it shouldn't take long for him to feel guilty. Of course she and I didn't discuss the eight-hundred-pound elephant in the room."

"Whether her brother was involved?" Chase guessed correctly. "I'm sure she's trying to put it out of her head as thoroughly as possible. It's her brother. She's not going to believe he had anything to do with Greg's death unless he confesses to it."

There were voices in the background of the call but Ellis couldn't make out what they were saying, only that they were feminine. Bailey and Willow must be listening in.

"Hold on one second, man. Okay, the ladies want to know if you've found Greg's wife yet. They want to make sure they're there for Peyton when that happens."

Ellis wanted to be there for her as well, but he'd come to terms with the fact he couldn't protect her from her late husband's past. "Not yet. Hopefully tomorrow. We have the address but we kind of got sidetracked with Jensen tonight. If he decides to talk tomorrow, that will take precedence over seeing the other family."

The other family.

It sounded so cold and clinical. Peyton had been handling every new revelation like a champ but how much more was she supposed to be able to take? Ellis was constantly second guessing their decision to come to London and meet the second wife. She might not have any helpful details regarding Greg's death or his involvement with Evandria, and Peyton would simply end up hurting for nothing.

"Any luck talking to your senator?" Ellis asked Chase. "Or Grant Hollister?"

"No one's heard from Grant since that note to Willow on the pizza receipt, which I guess is a good thing. He's under the radar and hopefully he's alive and safe. As for the senator, he's not returning my calls. Not a shock actually, considering the last time we talked to him he was sure Evandria hadn't done anything wrong. But I'll keep trying."

"Anything suspicious? Anything that you're worrying

about?"

Chase and Josh were charged with keeping Bailey and Willow safe, and from what Grant Hollister and Nigel Holmwood had told them that might be harder than it sounded.

"Nothing overt," Chase replied. "We're keeping to ourselves and staying out of sight for the most part. Josh did go into the office for a few hours today just to see if anyone was following him but he doesn't think anyone was watching. I have to say though, it might just be paranoia but I feel like we're being watched out here."

Ellis had the same hinky feeling, that crawling sensation on the back of his neck as if there were eyes everywhere. He'd felt it in Heathrow, he'd felt it in the lobby of the hotel, and had even felt it when they were walking down the street in Notting Hill.

"If you need to go underground, just go. You know how to get a message to me outside of the regular channels, right?"

"I do. I just hope we don't have to do it."

Ellis paused and checked to see if Peyton was still in the bathtub with the door shut. "Listen, I need to be quick here because Peyton will be out here any moment but I saw something in Jensen's apartment that I found intriguing. He had four gold coins framed and sitting on his mantle."

Chase whistled. "Now that is interesting. He's done the physical challenges that Josh and Willow learned about."

"So the next question is, were any of those challenges with Grant, Archer, Nigel, or hey, even the senator? Or maybe Stephen Baxter? Just how incestuous is this organization?"

There was silence for a long moment before Chase spoke. "You think Jensen had something to do with this, don't you?"

He'd thought of little else since he'd met Peyton's brother mere hours ago. "I think that I don't trust him. When someone lies to me about one thing, it makes me wonder what else he's lying about."

"Remember what Grant said," Chase reminded him. "Don't trust anyone."

It wasn't in Ellis's nature to trust or believe. He was trained to be skeptical and to verify whatever a suspect said. He believed in actions over words and thoughts. Sadly, he believed that the evil that one man could do to another was more horrific than most people could imagine, but he'd seen it in all its sickening glory.

Peyton believed in the innate goodness of mankind. Somehow, she even believed in him.

So for her, he'd give Jensen McMillen the benefit of the doubt. For now.

"DO YOU HAVE their address?" Ellis asked Peyton as they made their way out of the small cafe where they'd had breakfast and onto the sidewalk. The weather was typical for this time of the year, gray and rainy, making quite a contrast to the sun-drenched days they'd left behind, but at least the temperature was warm.

"Right here." She held up her phone, showing him a map of the city. "She doesn't live far."

Peyton had spent time in London over the past several years so he was depending on her to know her way around. "Should we get a taxi?"

"It's a quick tube ride," she said with a grin. "You don't mind rubbing elbows with the locals. do you?"

He preferred it. It was the best way to get to know a city. However, it might not be the safest, most controlled way to travel. "I think a taxi might be better. All those people around us are a threat."

He hated to say it out loud but the fact was the bigger crowd they were in, the more opportunity there was for something to go wrong.

Her smile fell. "I guess you're right."

"I wish I wasn't."

He stepped off of the curb to hail a taxi, Peyton right behind him. One of the iconic black taxicabs began to move toward them, slowing down as it approached. He and Peyton stepped forward just as the cab lunged forward, tires squealing and engine roaring. With only a split second to react, his adrenaline surged and he pushed Peyton backward, covering her body with his own. Grunting in pain, they landed on the unforgiving pavement with a thud, jarring every bone in his body as he tried to shield her from the impact as much as possible.

Managing to look up, he saw the vehicle veer back into the stream of traffic, quickly lost among the other ubiquitous taxis. Moving his arms and legs, he grimaced as a pain shot through his bruised side. He leaned back and inspected the shaken woman in his arms from head to toe, looking for any sign of injury. Just the thought of her being hurt again had him struggling to take a single breath.

"Are you okay?" he asked as he labored to his feet, helping

her as a crowd began to gather around them. She appeared to be unharmed but he had to be sure. "Are you hurt?"

"I'm fine, just startled. You have fast reflexes. We were almost roadkill," she said, her chest rising and falling rapidly. "Are you alright? You took the brunt of the fall."

"I've acquired a few new bruises but other than that I'm okay."

The onlookers were chattering, asking if they were hurt and if they needed a doctor. On high alert after what had happened, Ellis dispelled their fears and quickly pulled Peyton away from the crowd and down the street toward their hotel. The sooner he and she were in a controlled environment the better.

By some mutual agreement, neither said much until they were back inside the room. Ellis checked the suite while Peyton sank down onto the sofa in the sitting area. It was only when he joined her that he allowed himself to feel the full horror of what had almost transpired.

"I guess Evandria knows we're here," he finally said once his pulse rate was almost normal but his mind was still going a mile a minute as images of Peyton being hurt or killed rushed through his head.

Tucking her legs underneath her, Peyton let her head drop back on the cushions. "I guess they do. Hell of a welcome. I thought the British were supposed to be so nice and polite."

He laughed but it wasn't funny. "I don't think the Brits had anything to do with this. This was Evandria all the way."

She was quiet again, her gaze far away but where he didn't know. Perhaps back home in Midnight Blue Beach or maybe further than that...with Greg.

"I won't let anything happen to you, Peyton."

She nodded but didn't look his way. "I know what you're thinking."

That was a possibility. He was fairly single-minded these days.

"Then you know I'm thinking of ways to keep you safe."

Turning to him, he could see the tears in her sky blue eyes. "You're thinking it's a funny coincidence that we visited my brother last night and now I almost get run down."

He'd been thinking that too, but hadn't planned on making a big deal out of it. Not trusting people was par for the course for him and she shouldn't be surprised.

"What do you think?"

She rubbed the side of her face like a sleepy child who needed a nap. She probably was sick and tired of being a target. "I think it's a strange coincidence and I wonder who he's really loyal to. Our family or Evandria?"

"I don't have the answer for that," Ellis said truthfully. "That's something we already knew we needed to find out."

This time she looked him right in the eye, her mouth turned down and her expression unutterably sad. "I'm not sure I can handle it if I find out Jensen was involved in Greg's death. My own family…"

He moved closer and put an arm around her shoulders, careful not to get too personal. While they'd hugged and linked arms, even fallen asleep together on the couch, that didn't mean she wanted him to hold her in his arms. He'd never put her into an unwanted position.

"Let me tell you, Peyton Nelson, that I think you can handle a hell of a lot. You've had an amazing amount of garbage thrown at you in these last few weeks, including a package bomb that put you into a coma. You've held your head high and dealt with each new revelation as it was revealed. It might not be easy but I have no doubt you'll be fine in the end. You are a fierce warrior."

She didn't realize all the strength she carried inside of her. A lesser woman would have crumpled after all she'd been through.

"I hope you're right because I have a funny feeling things are going to get worse before they get better." The chime on her phone had her digging into her handbag. One look at the screen and she was groaning and rolling her eyes. "Wow, that came true fast."

He frowned, not sure what she was alluding to.

"Hi, Mom and Dad. How are things?"

Having met Peyton's mother and father, Ellis was sure of one thing. Nothing good could come from this. Her parents were toxic.

Chapter Three

B UFFY AND CHARLES McMillen were supposedly Peyton's parents but since she'd been a teenager, she hadn't been sure of that fact. While Jensen enjoyed the same things her mother and father did, she had always been the odd duck in the family.

Jensen had excelled at academics and couldn't wait to join one of the family businesses.

Peyton had been artsy and creative, wanting to be a photographer. She hadn't wanted anything to do with the family businesses, preferring instead to travel and see the world on a shoestring budget.

Her mother and father had despaired of Peyton ever "straightening up and assuming her responsibilities" which to her meant long, slow, agonizing torture by meetings and paperwork. She wanted to be outside, feeling the wind and sun on her face or feeling the raindrops on her skin. Being inside a classroom all day long had been unbearable.

So it was with great reluctance that Peyton climbed out of a taxi in front of her parents' London home. She'd had no idea that they were even here since the last time she saw them was in Williamsburg at the hospital. Usually they spent summers in Tuscany.

Ellis paid the driver. "Are you ready for this?"

Staring at the formal edifice, she couldn't help the sinking feeling in her stomach. She didn't know why she was being summoned but she had a feeling it was because Jensen had…tattled on her. He'd always done that when they were kids, telling her parents when she'd flunked a test or worn eyeshadow when she wasn't supposed to. He'd been a big pain in the ass and she'd hated that expression on his face when he told on her. So fucking morally superior. It was a miracle really that they were as close as they were now. Eventually she'd realized Jensen needed Buffy and Charles's approval much more than she did.

"Is it too late to make a run for it?" she joked, giving Ellis her best side-eye.

He shrugged and smiled. "I only have to outrun you and with my much longer legs it should be a piece of cake."

She placed her hand in the crook of his arm as they climbed the front steps. "But I'm highly motivated and I'd play dirty by tripping you."

"Yes, you would, princess, but I'm a cop. I'd be ready for it."

They stood at the front entrance, neither one reaching for the bell. Giggling at the absurdity of the situation, Peyton tried to school her features. Her parents weren't big on frivolity or happiness of any kind.

The butler must have been watching for her because the door swung open without the ring of the doorbell, and he silently stepped back so she and Ellis could enter. A shiver ran through her at the coldness of the furnishings even though the temperature in the home was warm. Peyton had only been in this house once about five years ago but it hadn't changed much. Vases worth tens of thousands of dollars, paintings that should have hung on a museum's walls, furniture that wasn't made to sit on.

"Your father is in the library," the uniformed man informed them, his British accent smooth but he didn't make eye contact, his gaze trained on an arrangement of roses on a round table. "Follow me, please."

"It's like Downton Abbey. I feel underdressed," Ellis whispered as they lagged behind the butler, but not too far. Peyton didn't remember where the library was located. Her parents had too many homes to keep them all straight.

"We are," Peyton agreed readily, her stomach churning as they ventured deeper into the house. "Even if we wore evening clothes, we would be dressed inappropriately. I gave up pleasing them years ago."

"It's fancy. I bet one of these paintings or sculptures is worth more than I make in a year."

He'd be right.

"Thanks for coming with me. I'm not looking forward to this."

"It's my job to protect you. You go nowhere without me."

The butler stopped in front of a set of oak double doors, knocking quietly. The gruff voice of her father could be heard through the heavy wood calling for them to come in. Before she could respond the butler was quickly gone, leaving them standing there all alone.

"Smart man," she muttered as she turned the doorknob, the

smell of her father's cigars bringing back many memories, most of them crappy.

"Peyton Elizabeth, are you coming in or not?"

Ah, the impatient tone of her dear old dad. That's something she couldn't hear enough.

"I'm right here, Dad. I hope we're not interrupting anything."

"Of course, you're not. I told you to be here at five for tea so why would I be doing anything else? You're late. And what do you mean by *we*?"

Peyton wondered if she was supposed to apologize for being late first or answer his question. She decided to ignore his query.

"The taxi got caught in traffic but we're here only five minutes late."

"Your tardiness puts the cook off her timing, Peyton Elizabeth. It's very selfish to think only of yourself. You should have left earlier to ensure that you were on time."

I should have run when I had the chance.

"Sorry, Father. We left in plenty of time actually, but as I said the traffic was bad. London and all that."

Charles grunted, his eyes narrowing as he took in his daughter and her companion. After all these years she still felt like a naughty child in the principal's office, she could only imagine how Ellis felt at the moment.

One glance at the man next to her showed a different story though. He seemed completely unperturbed by her father's affectations and general surliness. Maybe because he could out surly anyone anywhere? Or maybe because he truly didn't give a shit about Charles McMillen. Those people were few and far between but she treasured them as if they were gold.

"Well, come in then and sit down. Your mother might be joining us later. Now didn't I tell you to come alone? Who is this?"

She and Ellis settled on the damask covered settee kitty-corner to her father's oversized leather chair by the fireplace which this time of the year sat empty.

"I told you I have a friend with me. This is Detective Ellis Hunter from Virginia. I'm sure you remember him from the hospital."

From the thin white line around her father's lips she had a feeling he was none too happy.

Oh well. Peyton could only remember making her father truly happy once, and now even that had a whole new connotation. She might even ask him about that today if she could work it into the conversation.

Charles looked good for a man in his early sixties. His hair was gray but his body was in good shape due to workouts three times a week plus as much golf as he could fit into his schedule. He hadn't slowed down much in his late years, still in control of several companies. Peyton had assumed he might hand over some of the control to Jensen, but so far he didn't seem in any hurry to do that. He would probably go into the great hereafter at his desk.

"It's very nice to see you again, sir," Ellis said, extending his hand. Charles stared at it a second or two too long but did eventually rise slightly from his chair and shake Ellis's hand.

A young maid bustled into the library at that moment, setting out an elaborate tea service on the large round coffee table.

When she was finished, she left as quietly as she'd entered.

Her father cleared his throat. "Your mother isn't here to pour, Peyton Elizabeth."

Peyton hadn't poured at a formal tea since her cotillion days but she'd try. Studiously keeping her hands from shaking, she served three cups of tea in tiny, fragile porcelain so delicate she could see the shadow of her hand through them. Finger sandwiches and small tarts were served on little plates, and by the time she was finished pouring she'd worked up something of an appetite.

"So you called me, Father?"

A sidelong glance at Ellis before Charles answered. "I did, young lady. It seems we have something to discuss but this is family matters." A more pointed look at Ellis this time. "Private matters."

"He's here to protect me."

Charles waved at Ellis. "Yes, yes, that's what you said and what Jensen told me. But what's going to happen to you in your own parents' home? He can wait in the kitchen with the cook."

Her father was often insufferably rude to people and he was doing it again. Her cheeks burned with embarrassment at how Ellis was being treated. "Father, you're not being very polite–"

Ellis stood, his hand on Peyton's shoulder. "Actually, I think that's a good idea. I'll give you two a chance to talk. Where is the kitchen?"

Scowling, Charles took a sip of his tea. "I have no idea, young man, but I'm sure someone as industrious as you are can find it."

She would have given her father a blistering reply but Ellis's hand tightened slightly in warning. She'd cautioned him about her dad and he'd replied that he didn't want to get into it with the old man. Ellis assured her that he wouldn't be an extra irritant to Charles McMillen since she was probably already in trouble about Evandria.

He gave her a reassuring smile. "I'll be back in a little while."

She had no business feeling abandoned but she'd grown used to having Ellis at her side almost twenty-four seven. It was strange when he wasn't there. But Charles had a point; no harm was going to come to her in the library of her parents' home, especially with Ellis only a few feet away.

She'd learned a great deal about Detective Ellis Hunter in the last few weeks and she'd bet he wasn't going to the kitchen right now. Instead, he was going to prowl around the house checking for people watching them. He was a cop through and through.

"So now will you tell me what you wanted?" she asked when Ellis was gone. "Why I was summoned today?"

Her father harrumphed and put down his tea cup, reaching for the whiskey on the small table next to him. "You act as if seeing your family is some sort of imposition, Peyton Elizabeth."

Controlling the laughter that bubbled up at his words, she didn't take the bait. "You asked to see me. Now I'm here."

"What is that man doing in London with you?"

Was this what her father wanted? To talk about Ellis?

"He's protecting me," she said again. "There have been a couple attempts on my life, first in Williamsburg and now here in London."

That captured her father's attention. "Here? When did that

happen?"

"This morning. A taxi tried to run myself and Ellis down."

Charles always looked unhappy but his expression was thunderous at her statement.

"Did you call Scotland Yard?"

"What's the point? We can't prove it and the taxi was quickly lost in a sea of them. There's not much to be done."

Leaning forward in his chair, his eyes narrowed to slits. "Seems like this detective isn't doing such a great job of protecting you."

"I'm alive, aren't I?" she shot back. "He's doing a fine job. I do notice though that you haven't asked me why I believe my life is in danger, so I assume you've talked to Jensen. My dearest brother never could keep a secret."

"Jensen is a fine son to call and let us know what's been going on with you—otherwise we might never have found out."

Inwardly rolling her eyes, Peyton had to control the stream of sarcasm that was waiting to come out of her mouth. "Now you know. But I think the real question is more like…how long have you known? Did you know Greg was in Arsenal? Did you know that he had another family here in London?"

Charles McMillen's expression gave nothing away but that wasn't a shock. He was a master businessman, used to hiding his thoughts and feelings.

"I had no idea Greg had volunteered for Arsenal nor did I know about his other family. I would never have approved of you staying married to him if I'd had that knowledge."

She found that difficult if not impossible to believe. Her father had put Greg Nelson in her path for one reason and one reason only. To be her lawfully wedded husband. It had sealed a huge merger between Greg's parents' company and Charles's. Their children had simply been the pawns in the business deal.

"Are you sure, Dad? Because you were desperate for me to marry Greg and when I talked about divorcing him you were desperate for me to *stay* married to him. In fact, I think you loved Greg more than I did. Maybe you should have married him."

"I didn't hear you complaining much when you two met. You thought he was wonderful and couldn't wait to tie the knot, if I recall."

She remembered it too but things hadn't turned out like she'd hoped. "You made sure I did. He was sold to me as the anti-you. He was free-spirited, creative, and openly scornful of conspicuous consumption. What I didn't know was that he was an irresponsible asshole who drank, womanized, and gambled his way through Europe. But I'm guessing you knew he was like that before you ever introduced us."

"You give me too much credit, Peyton Elizabeth. I only wanted what was best for you and I thought a husband would help you settle down. You didn't seem to know what you wanted to do with your life. Marrying Greg gave you purpose."

It sure as fuck did. Keeping her husband alive after too many bottles of wine or losing too much money at the casino made sure her days were filled.

"And look how that turned out," she said, her tone hard. "A disaster."

Her father had the nerve to nod and agree. "It was. There's a pattern there though. Everything you touch seems to go in the wrong direction. Your mother and I are offering to get you back on the right track. Forget this vendetta about Evandria and Greg. He's gone and nothing can bring him back. There's a place for you in any of my businesses. Just pick one and it's yours."

Jumping to her feet, she turned her back on her father, walking to the wall of bookshelves and pretending to peruse the titles. Anger burned in her gut but she wouldn't give him the satisfaction of letting him know he'd got to her. That's all he truly wanted. The offer to give her a company was bullshit. If she called his bluff he'd never do it. If he hadn't given one to Jensen, he sure as hell wasn't going to do it for her, his *flighty* daughter.

"I'm not sure how my lousy marriage was my fault when you picked my husband, Father. But I've already found his killer. Archer Caldwell killed Greg along with several others. He did it for the power. So my next question probably seems obvious. You're a member of Evandria and you have been for years. What side are you on in the war?"

Laughter. Her father's deep laughter reached her ears and had her turning around to face him. He looked amused as if she'd told a ribald joke.

"Darling, there is no war. There is always a struggle when it comes to power, but a war? You always were so dramatic."

"Then why did Grant Hollister and Nigel Holmwood both say that me and my friends are caught in the middle of a battle? That our lives were in danger and we needed to leave Midnight Blue Beach? Were they just playing with us? Just joking around?"

Charles shook his head before draining his glass. "I've never even heard those names, Peyton. But if I ever do meet them I'll be quite angry that they've filled your head with nonsense. What happened to you at the hotel in Williamsburg was an accident. An explosion meant for someone else. You were in the wrong place at the wrong time."

"And the taxi this morning?"

"The drivers in this city are simply crazy. Dangerous but it had nothing to do with you."

She smiled as she thought of the word she was about to use. The word they'd all come to hate.

"It was all a coincidence then?"

He smiled as much as he was capable. "That's it. Just a coincidence."

"Like how Greg died on the same exact day as Frank Scott and Alex Vaughn?"

The smile faded but she pressed on.

"Like how Stephen Baxter died even though the doctors said he was getting better. Like how a car bomb went off in Midnight Blue Beach, blowing up Nigel Holmwood's car. And let's not forget that Roy's Bar was set on fire because I was going to meet Grant Hollister there and he was going to give us the evidence that Archer Caldwell had killed our husbands. Shall I go on, Father? Because that's one hell of a lot of coincidences. I didn't even mention how Greg was killed on the anniversary of the birth of Evandria. That's strange, don't you think?"

Her words dripped with acid but Charles appeared unmoved and unamused. In other words, his everyday expression.

"You're overwrought but if you truly believe that you are in danger I'll hire a twenty-four-hour security firm. The best in the business. Much better than that small town cop that's been following you around. He can go home."

She looked her father straight in the eye. "You don't like Ellis because you didn't pick him out personally."

"And you like him because I don't. Do you honestly think you could make a relationship with him work, Peyton Elizabeth? You were born for better things…better men."

She sucked in a breath at how heartless and snobby her father could be. "He's the best man I've ever known. Ever."

She said the last word with emphasis, wanting to be sure he knew her meaning. Ellis was the best man she'd ever met including Charles McMillen.

"You believe that now but your judgment has never been the best. Come home and we'll set everything to rights. Leave Evandria alone. It's not responsible for your life, you are."

Whirling around, she headed straight for the library door. She'd had enough familial love for the day. "I'm going to find out who tried to blow me up. I'm going to find out who ordered Archer Caldwell to kill Greg, Alex, and Frank. I'm going to find out who wants to kill me now. I can do it with your help or without it. It's up to you."

"Foolish child," her father jeered as she jerked the door open. "Nothing is as you think it is. But even if it was, you think you could bring down Evandria? That's a pipe dream. It has power that you can't even begin to imagine."

"You always accused me of being a dreamer," she said as she breezed out of the room, almost running right into someone. Stepping back, Peyton realized it was her mother.

"Leaving so soon?" Buffy McMillen said, glancing into the library and then back at Peyton. "Why don't you come out to the garden and we'll chat?"

It wasn't a request but a command. This time Peyton didn't argue or fight it. She needed to find out what her mother knew about Evandria and why she'd kept her daughter from joining.

Chapter Four

BUFFY'S FINGERS CARESSED the velvety petal of a crimson rose. Dressed in a pale pink Chanel pantsuit she was the epitome of class, style, and old money. She was the quintessential corporate spouse, always putting her husband first, while simultaneously throwing lavish parties.

Peyton hoped she would age as gracefully. Her mother looked years younger than her actual age with stylish blonde hair, a trim figure, and well-cared for skin.

"The blooms turned out especially lovely this year. I rarely get to see them as we're usually in Tuscany. I'll have one of the maids cut a bouquet for you," Buffy said, cutting a flower from the bush.

Peyton sat down on one of the padded lounge chairs situated in the middle of the garden under a vine trellis. "I don't have anything to put them in, Mother. We're staying at a hotel."

"You should just stay here. We have plenty of room."

Not a chance in hell.

"We're fine where we are, but thank you for the offer. Honestly, I don't think Father would like Ellis staying here."

Her mother came to sit next to Peyton, a rose in her hand. "I can handle your father."

"You don't need to do that. We're quite settled into the hotel and it's a nice place. We all just argue when we're together."

Buffy smiled at Peyton's honesty. "We weren't the right parents for you, were we? You needed a different type of mother and father, the kind that snuggled and read bedtime stories."

Peyton couldn't imagine her mother and father doing any of that even on their last day on earth. "The nanny read to me."

Brows up, Buffy looked surprised. "Really? Which one?"

"All of them, Mother. At least until I was a proficient reader on my own."

Buffy should never have had children. She didn't even know that reading bedtime stories was a normal occurrence. But then Peyton often wondered at her own mother's upbringing and if it had been as cold and sterile as her own. Maybe it was all she knew.

"Well done, then. I chose my employees well," her mother congratulated herself. "Now tell me about this threat on your life, Peyton, and what you're doing to protect yourself. Jensen said you're in great danger from Evandria."

"Father thinks I've made all this up," Peyton retorted. "That my head is filled with fairy tales."

Sitting back in the chair, Buffy folded her hands together on her lap. "If you believe it, then I believe it."

This was new. Her mother was being…supportive? Had she started drinking or something?

"I know it's true. Some cabbie tried to run me down this morning and you know about the package bomb. Plus, there have been other incidents. I found out Archer Caldwell killed Greg, Frank, and Alex but I don't know who ordered him to. Evandria doesn't want me to find out."

"This was why I wanted you kept out of that organization," Buffy said, shaking her head, lips in a tight line. "I never liked those men that Charles would spend time with. They all seemed power hungry to me, and rather arrogant. I thought the same about Archer whenever I was around him. I thought he could be ruthless if he wanted something."

For some reason Peyton was surprised that her mother knew Caldwell. "How long have you known Archer?"

"For years. We all travel in the same social circles."

"Then you know Nigel Holmwood and Grant Hollister?"

Peyton hadn't forgotten her father had denied knowing them, which had to be bullshit.

"We've met many members over the years. Are they important?"

Nodding, Peyton wondered how much to tell her mother and what Buffy McMillen already knew. "They both think that myself and my friends are caught in the middle of a war for power in the organization. Mother, you deliberately kept me out of Evandria?"

"I did and I'm not sorry. I saw how petty they all were, always fighting amongst themselves about officer elections and department appointments. You would have never been interested in anything like that. To them it's all about the money, something you don't care about either. I thought the perfect compromise was to have you marry someone in the organization. You were a part of it without being official. You got to keep your freedom to do whatever you wanted."

It made sense. Peyton wouldn't have cared about Evandria although the young, idealistic girl she'd been years ago might have been drawn in by their mission to make the world a better place rhetoric.

"What about their philanthropic works?" Peyton asked. "Did you think I'd be interested in that?"

Buffy's lips turned up at the corners but it was a cold smile, the kind that didn't speak of happiness or cheer. "You weren't even interested in being our child, let alone joining a club of rich people who wanted to change the world. Evandria didn't have what you wanted. Freedom."

Peyton couldn't stop herself from asking the question, although she was sure she knew the answer. "What about you, Mother? Did you get what you wanted?"

"Yes, I did," Buffy answered simply but didn't expound on the reply. "Now, are you and your young man going to stay for dinner? We're having duck."

Shaking her head, Peyton decided to ask one more question. "Thank you but we can't. Mother, did you know Greg had another family?"

If it was possible, her mother's icy blue gaze turned even chillier, almost silver. "If I had known he would have regretted that decision. He brought shame not only to you and himself but his family, friends, and Evandria. You're better off without him. You need to find another man to spend your life with. Someone stronger than Greg and with more integrity."

That was the most emotion Buffy had shown in years. But then Greg's actions also reflected on the McMillen family as well. That wouldn't go over well with Buffy and Charles.

"Maybe," Peyton conceded. "Men like that don't grow on trees from my experience."

Although Ellis had integrity in spades. But the timing sucked. Now wasn't the most opportune moment to start a romance.

Standing, her mother beckoned to Peyton instead of grilling her about Ellis. "Come with me, please."

Following, they went into the house and crossed over into a small sitting room that clearly belonged to her mother. In the corner was a small, old-fashioned roll top desk. Buffy opened it and retrieved a set of keys and an envelope before handing both items to Peyton.

"I want you to take these." Buffy pressed the keys into Peyton's palm, the metal of the keychain cold against her skin. "They belong to an old family house that I inherited from my late uncle, Earnest Gable. Even your father doesn't know about this place. The house isn't fancy but it is unknown and if you need a place to hide, it might fit the bill."

Staring at the keys, Peyton wasn't sure she was hearing her mother correctly. "You believe me, then? That Evandria is trying to kill me, or at least scare me?"

"If you believe it, then I believe it," her mother repeated. "I may not be good at reading bedtime stories but I can and will protect my only daughter. But I will say this—whatever it is you're seeking by finding out who had Greg killed, assuming that you're right and it was murder, it won't change anything. He'll still be gone and you'll have to come to grips with the secrets that you've unearthed. For all you know, there might be more to come and they could be much worse. Don't let him control your life all these years later. Maybe it's time to just move on and put this behind you."

Every cell in Peyton's body rejected her mother's words. "Isn't the truth important? Wouldn't you want to know?"

"Happiness doesn't hinge on the truth, Peyton. Some of the happiest people I know don't have a clue what's going on around them but they don't care. They're happy and that's enough. You may find that you can't have it both ways. Uncovering the truth may only cause heartache and sadness."

"I've thought about that but I'm willing to take that risk."

Buffy gave her a shrewd look. "And there's no way I can talk you out of this?"

Peyton shook her head. "No, I'm doing it."

"Then definitely take the keys and the house deed. You might find you need it. Knowing what little I do about Evandria, if what you say is true, they're not going to take you digging into their affairs well." Her mother's gaze moved from Peyton to the doorway. "And there's your young man. It looks like he's ready to go. Come see us again before we leave."

Ellis was standing in the doorway looking way past ready to leave and wearing an expression that she'd come to recognize.

He wanted to talk to her.

"Thank you again, Mother." Her fingers tightened on the keys and envelope. "But you're right, we have another engagement."

They didn't but the excuse of a social commitment was something that Buffy understood. Peyton linked her arm with Ellis's as they exited the house and walked down the pavement to look for a taxi. She couldn't wait any longer now that they were out of hearing distance of the house.

"You want to tell me something. I can see it in your face. Did you overhear something my father said after I left his study?"

Grinning wickedly, Ellis hailed a taxi and bundled her inside before he answered. "I didn't hear a thing, princess, but I found out all I needed to before I even left you two alone."

He was enjoying this. Dragging it out.

"Spill it," she commanded, her patience short after a visit with her parents. She was never in the best of moods after an afternoon spent in their company. "Don't make me knee you in the balls, mister."

Laughing, Ellis crossed his legs. "Ouch. You're a mean one when you're around mummy and daddy. Did you see the photographs in your father's study? The ones on the shelves behind him?"

Ellis was a well-trained cop. He saw everything, even the smallest details.

"No, I didn't even notice they were there."

"That's because you were looking at your father not at his surroundings, while I was doing the opposite. But there was a photo just behind your father in a silver frame. He was in a golf foursome – himself, Holmwood, Caldwell, and some man I didn't recognize. Daddy dearest definitely knows Archer and Nigel. I'm not shocked since your father's been an officer of the organization."

Charles McMillen had lied.

That wasn't a shock either.

Chapter Five

BACK AT THE hotel, Peyton was working on the names and addresses Willow had found in her husband's statue while Ellis studied the latest information Chase and Josh had sent over regarding Evandria. While there had been no official announcement regarding Archer Caldwell being replaced as president of the organization, there did appear to be some harried movement among the members. No one was answering their calls to meet and the security around The Retreat had increased to black-helicopter-paranoia levels. More cameras, more guards, and more scrutiny. Josh and Willow had returned to check out what might be happening in the area and had seen it for themselves. The Retreat was on lockdown.

Ellis assumed that was where Holmwood had taken Caldwell so it made sense. They had a multiple murderer on their hands who had nothing to lose. Keeping the residents of the area safe would be a priority.

Keeping Peyton safe was Ellis's priority. She'd shown him the keys and deed to her mother's secret home near Midnight Blue Beach. He'd sent on the information to Josh and Chase so they could check it out but it might be a good place for all of them to lie low for awhile when he and Peyton returned to the States. He wasn't sure what had prompted her mother to tell them about it but he wasn't about to look a gift horse in the mouth when one trotted into the living room. The safer he could keep the women, the more freedom they had to investigate.

"Shit, shit, shit," Peyton muttered, tapping the pen on the paper in front of her. She was sitting at the little desk in the corner of the suite, leaning her head on her hand.

"Problem?"

Twisting in the chair, she sent him a glare but the anger wasn't directed at him. If she had access to matches she would have set that paper on fire.

"Nothing is working," she huffed, her shoulders slumping. "I'm getting frustrated."

He put down his phone and crossed the short distance to where she was sitting. "There might not be any code. You've made a huge assumption here that these names and addresses have some other meaning than the obvious. If you can't figure it out, it just might be because there is nothing there."

"There has to be something," she argued, frustration wrinkling her forehead. "It's too weird that the addresses don't even exist and yet this piece of paper was put in a safe place. Why would Alex Vaughn keep a list of names and addresses hidden if they weren't important? If I had a list that was wrong, I'd throw it in the trash. There has to be more to this."

He couldn't argue the logic but this case had been so strange from the get-go he couldn't rule anything out. "Let's think about this then. What have you tried so far?"

Letting out a slow breath, she moved the paper so he could easily see it, pointing out the first name and address combination. "I tried the obvious ones, of course. Reversing the letters? That was obviously a bust. Then I tried every second letter or every third letter and so on. No luck. Then I tried the old letters-for-numbers in forward and reverse but that didn't work either. So now I'm working on a cipher text but it's going to take some time. I have to look at the letter substitution patterns one at a time. Sometimes they're easy, like the most common letter is usually 'E' so I would look for the most common letter in these addresses and use that as the substitute, but sometimes they even change them mid-cipher. It's enough to give you a headache and I already have one of those."

Ellis was impressed. "How did you learn this? It's not something I would expect the daughter of a billionaire to know."

A brow arched and she grinned. "Are you kidding? I used my very own cipher text to communicate with my secret high school boyfriend. The school I went to was beyond strict and if they'd found those letters I would have been in big trouble. This way they just thought it was gibberish. I told them I was practicing my handwriting. They bought it."

She was full of surprises and it only made him more attracted to her. How she had survived so well with parents like Buffy and Charles McMillen he'd never know. "I bow down to the master. If that doesn't work out, what else is there?"

"Google," she answered with no hesitation. "When I said I was good at puzzles, I meant it, but this might be beyond what a teenage girl at a strict boarding school would know."

"I read once that during the Cold War the CIA would use

their shoelaces to communicate messages. Different tying methods meant different things."

She glanced down at her bare feet. "Is that supposed to help or is that just one of your handy-dandy factoids?"

Chuckling, Ellis eased the pen from her fingers and set it on the desk, then wrapped an arm around her waist and lifted her to her feet. She needed to take a break and she must have agreed because she didn't fight him.

"A little of both. I'm just saying that whatever the code is, it may be something so wacky no one could figure it out. Now it's time to leave it alone for awhile. You said your head hurts and that means you need to rest. Do you want one of your pills?"

She hated taking them, saying they made her sleepy but he couldn't stand to see her in any pain. "No, I'd rather just take some ibuprofen. I don't want to fall asleep yet."

He headed for the bathroom, giving her a nudge toward the couch he'd just vacated. "Make yourself comfortable and I'll go get them."

"You don't have–"

"I know," he said, not letting her finish. What she didn't seem to understand was that he liked taking care of her. It must have happened very little in her adult life because she was incredibly grateful for every tiny thing he did. "But you need to rest."

He came back out with two tablets and she quickly downed them with the last of her bottle of water, while he settled at the end of the couch, her feet in his lap. "Thank you."

"You're welcome. I also ordered dinner so it should be here any minute. I thought you might have worked up an appetite while wrestling with those addresses."

"You're going to make someone a good wife one day," she giggled, the sound making his heart skip a beat in his chest. This woman didn't have any idea how she affected him.

Placing his hand over his heart, he sighed. "That's all I've ever dreamed about."

Reaching out with one shapely leg encased in sweatpants, she nudged his shoulder. "You think you're so funny."

"I know I'm funny. There's a difference. Just don't tell anyone, okay? I've got them all sold on this irritable detective persona. They think that's what I'm really like."

Peyton rolled her lovely blue eyes. "Trust me. That's what you're really like. Most of the time. The rest of the time you're pretty human." She leaned forward so they were almost nose to nose. "But you are no comedian. Give it up, Detective."

"I just don't have much patience with stupid people."

Or people in his way to getting something done. People who only thought about themselves. People who parked poorly at the grocery store. People who asked him to fill out some kind of form. People who drove after drinking. People who get to the order box at a drive thru and still don't know what they want despite waiting in line for ten minutes.

"Just stupid people?" Peyton snorted. "Are you sure it's not more?"

Clearing his throat, he went back to the messages on his phone. "Just stupid people."

It was a small lie but she already knew the truth. They'd spent virtually every hour of the day together since she'd been in the hospital. She just didn't remember some of it.

"If you say so."

It was the tone in her voice that didn't sound quite right. Putting down his phone, he gave her all of his attention.

"What's wrong?"

"You don't like stupid people."

She was going somewhere with this but damned if he knew the destination.

"Can you cut to the chase? What's on that mind of yours?"

Sitting up, she pulled her feet in and wrapped her arms around her legs, resting her chin on her knees. "Do you think I'm stupid?"

"No, I don't, but I'm guessing that you think you might be. Am I right?"

"You've met my parents and my brother. You know some of my marriage to Greg. It's enough to make a judgment."

Ahh, that word. Judgment. She wanted to beat herself up and she wanted him to help. Not going to happen. "I'm a cop, not a judge. I gather the evidence and let it fall where it may."

"But you have opinions," she persisted. "Do you think I'm stupid?"

Far from it, actually. "I think you're a survivor and you should be proud of yourself. I think the work that you, Bailey, and Willow have done is nothing short of phenomenal. I think you were born into the wrong family and had lousy fucking parents. I think your brother is a jerk and I think your late husband was a complete and total asshole who thought about nothing but himself. I also think you've made some bad decisions, starting with marrying Greg and then staying with him when he proved to be a dirtbag. But none of that makes you stupid."

Tears glittered in his eyes and now he felt like a shmuck. The last thing he'd wanted to do was upset her. She was supposed to be resting.

"Sometimes I feel like an idiot," she whispered, her face half-buried in her folded arms. "I think about the might-have-beens."

Ellis wasn't a man that allowed himself to think about regrets. He had them of course, all human beings did, but if he gave them too much space in his head then they crowded out all the good things about the here and now.

"Like what?" he asked, turning on the cushion so they were facing each other, their toes inches apart.

"If I hadn't married Greg I might have made photography my career."

"Your parents would have hated that."

Her shoulders shook with laughter. "They would have. I never would have heard the end of it. I guess I wasn't strong enough to go against the tide."

The last fucking thing Ellis wanted to talk about was her douchebag husband but it looked like she was wallowing in doubts and maybes.

"Did you love the bastard?"

He thought she'd answer right away but she took her time before speaking. "Yes and no. I loved what he represented to me but when I look back I think the answer is no. I didn't love Greg."

Something shifted in Ellis's chest, tightening his rib cage and making it hard to catch his breath. "What did he represent?"

She smiled. "Freedom. Freedom from my parents."

"Did it work?"

Nodding, she wiped at her eye where a tear was beginning to fall. "To an extent, it did. But then they pushed a new agenda on me."

"Grandchildren?"

The thought of Peyton having a baby for that clown only made Ellis more irritable. Greg hadn't deserved her loyalty and care.

Her brows shot up. "Funny, they never bugged me about that. I always assumed it was because deep down they didn't really like children. No, they wanted me to work for one of the family businesses. They were constantly harping about that."

Ellis hated to burst her bubble but that seemed to be his designated job these days.

"Or they knew he was in Arsenal and wasn't even supposed to get married in the first place."

"Or that," she agreed. "We know that my father lied about Nigel and Archer. Everybody lied, Ellis. Even me."

He scooted closer and reached for her hands, so cold to the touch, and warmed them up with his own. "What did you lie about, princess?"

"That I was happy."

"Maybe when this is all over and you're not in danger anymore, you can be happy then."

Her gaze was warm and soft, and he had to resist the urge to lean forward and kiss her. She'd never invited that sort of attention from him.

"I'm happy now," she said, her voice stronger than before. "I'm not waiting to be anything anymore. Finally, I'm standing on my own two feet and getting the truth. That makes me happy. It's the lying that made me miserable."

He'd do whatever he could to make sure she stayed that way.

Chapter Six

THEY LOOKED LIKE a happy family. The mother appeared to be a few years younger than Peyton, although guessing ages wasn't an exact science. Tall and willowy with auburn hair and pale skin, the woman was the physical opposite of Peyton. When choosing a second wife, Greg must have gone for a different model.

Ellis glanced down at the paper from the Evandria file. "Her name is Amelia and she's thirty-two years old. The kids, Noelle and Andrew, are nine and seven."

That would have made Amelia incredibly young and naive when she'd met Greg. Peyton felt a surge of sympathy for the other woman. Amelia had trusted Greg and he'd left her with two children and little else.

Hidden behind a tree where the trio couldn't see them, Peyton studied the children for any sign of Greg. From all appearances, they took after their mother in coloring but she thought she could see their father's eyes and chin on the diminutive faces.

The girl had her nose in a book and the boy was riding his

bicycle in circles around his little family, laughing and smiling the entire time. The mother had bent down to speak to the little girl and the child nodded in understanding. They took off down the street, probably toward the park that wasn't far away.

"Let's follow them," Peyton said impulsively. "I'd like to see more, and yes, I'm well aware that our watching them is creepy."

"You're thinking about giving a woman you've never met millions of dollars. I think that's reason enough to want to get to know her a little."

Peyton was past thinking about it. Greg had blown pretty much all of his money except for his yearly trust fund but she had money of her own. His children shouldn't suffer because their father was an irresponsible jerk.

They took off behind the woman and her children but kept their distance, not wanting to bring attention to themselves. The family did indeed go to the park and the little boy took off, circling a large flower bed while the mother and daughter unfolded a blanket and sat down on the lush grass. Peyton and Ellis hung back watching the family interact for quite awhile.

"Are you going to talk to her?" Ellis finally asked, his voice low as they stood behind a large fountain. "I can distract the children."

She'd been wondering about that very question. It's what she'd come to London for but now that the moment was here…

She couldn't do it.

It wasn't that she was afraid, because she wasn't. It wasn't that she held anger or resentment toward Amelia. She didn't.

It was because they looked happy. Content with their lives. They didn't need Peyton coming out of the woodwork all this time later and dredging up the past. It was bad enough the she was having to relive it because of all that they'd uncovered in the last weeks, but dragging this woman into it wasn't going to make things any better. Peyton didn't want to hurt Amelia or her children.

Placing her hand on Ellis's arm, she smiled at the younger boy's antics, racing faster and faster around the circle. "I'm going to leave them in peace."

He tucked a strand of hair behind her ear. "They might have information that could help us."

She nodded. "They might but it's not worth it. They're innocent in all of this and they don't need me throwing their lives into chaos. Especially those kids. I can't do that to them just because I need answers to move on. Look at them, Ellis. They already have."

Standing behind her, his hands rested on her shoulders. She could feel the warmth of his skin through the thin cotton of her blouse and she let herself lean back on him, feeling the strength he offered freely and without reservation. Since she'd met this man, he'd been there for her every moment of every day and had asked for nothing in return except one thing. To trust him. Now she had to trust herself and what her gut was telling her. Leave this family alone.

"I think you're a good woman, Peyton Nelson."

She looked up at him smiling down on her. "I'd like to think any decent human being would do the same."

"Sadly we have a severe shortage of those lately."

"Are you mad at me? I know you were hoping she had information that would help us."

He dropped a kiss on the crown of her head like she was one of the children who played here in the park. He'd never pushed her, never gotten too close, respecting her boundaries. But the distance that had seemed so important even a few days ago didn't feel all that necessary anymore. Ellis was nothing like Greg. If she let him in, he wasn't going to hurt her that way. Not on purpose.

"Then we'll find another way to get what we need. We'll go back and talk to your brother. We both know he knows more than what he's told us. Hell, we don't have to even talk to him. I can tail him and see where he goes and who he talks to. I can also get my FBI buddy to dig into his past business dealings. We might find something there."

Peyton thought about her friends back in Williamsburg. They were waiting for news of this meeting and now she'd called it off. "The others might not understand."

Ellis shrugged. "Then we'll make them understand. Don't second guess yourself, Peyton. You've made the call."

But did I do the right thing?

She wanted answers so desperately but there were limits as to what she'd do to get them. She'd found one of those limits today.

"I'm glad I was able to see them, though. It does give me a sort of closure. I want them to be happy. This wasn't their fault."

"You're a better person than I am."

"I'm really not," she denied with a snort. "I highly doubt Amelia knew Greg was already married when she married him. If anything, she's a victim."

"And Greg is a douche."

That made her laugh despite the seriousness of the moment.

"And Greg is a douche," she repeated. "I married a douche and I'm not very proud of myself."

Ellis moved restlessly behind her. "Cut yourself some slack. You were young, just like Amelia. Plus, your parents and all that mess. You married the wrong person. It's a big, non-exclusive club, princess."

Stepping out from behind the fountain, she watched as the little boy named Andrew zipped around on his bicycle, up and down the paths. When she'd been married to Greg, she hadn't wanted a baby. After all, Greg had been infantile and taking care of him took up a great deal of her time, but seeing these children and their smiling mother made her wonder if perhaps she'd missed out.

"It's not too late."

Jumping at the sound of Ellis's voice, she whirled around to face him. "You scared me. I thought you were still over there."

"Where you go, I go. I meant what I said. You're still young. It's not too late."

"I don't know what you're talking about."

His laugh was deep and warm. "You have a terrible poker face. Every thought you have is written all over it. But go ahead and pretend you don't know what I'm talking about. Now, are you ready to go? We need to talk about what we're going to do next."

Now that I've blown this lead.

She took his arm and they headed back down the path toward the street where they could catch a taxi. That route took them right by Amelia and Noelle but they didn't notice Peyton and Ellis. Andrew zoomed around the flower circle again but this time his tire skidded and he began to slide, the bike tilting precariously to one side. With lightning reflexes, Ellis was there in a second, grabbing the handlebars to keep the bike from hitting the ground and helping the little boy off when it finally came to a halt.

Amelia gave a cry of alarm and sprinted over to her son, the daughter on her heels. "Andy, are you alright? I told you not to go that fast around the corners."

Ellis patted the young man on the shoulder. "I think he's okay."

For a moment Peyton wanted to flee but then she reminded herself that this woman had no idea who she was or that they had been watching the family. They would simply be American strangers who had done a good deed for the day. Strangers they would stay.

Andrew jumped into his mother's arms. "I'm not hurt. I promise."

Amelia checked her son from head to toe before turning to Peyton and Ellis. "Thank you so much for–"

Her voice trailed off and her eyes had gone wide. She was staring at Peyton as if she'd seen a ghost. Her throat worked and her mouth moved but only a squeak came out.

"Ma'am, is everything okay?" Ellis asked, an alarmed glance in Peyton's direction. Suddenly it didn't seem out of the realm of possibility that Amelia had indeed known about Greg's other life. Her status as a victim was looking shaky and Peyton felt a rush of anger sweep through her like a red tide. What kind of woman would marry a man already married?

Amelia shook her head and rubbed at her eyes, her chest rising and falling rapidly.

"I'm sorry," her voice came out breathless and thin. "It's just…you look very like someone."

Ellis had a hand on Peyton's arm and the fingers tightened fractionally at the woman's statement. Her own heart was beating loudly against her ribs. If this woman wasn't as innocent as Peyton had believed, then maybe talking to her wasn't the horrible, intrusive thing she'd thought it was.

"Who did you think I was?" Peyton asked. It took all her effort to keep the emotion out of her voice that was currently threatening to overwhelm her.

Amelia didn't answer, instead bending down and speaking quietly to her children who then bounded away to the blanket where there was water and snacks.

"I'm sorry," she apologized again, glancing over her shoulder where the kids were sitting. "You look like the late wife of my husband. She was an American too."

"Your husband?" Ellis asked sharply, his gaze darting around. "Is he here as well?"

Her cheeks colored and her lips turned down. "My *late* husband, actually. Now if you'll excuse me I need to get back to my children. Good day and thank you again."

Amelia turned to go but Peyton couldn't allow this moment to end. Greg had told her his wife was *dead* but she was very much alive and pissed off. All the reasons she'd planned to walk away had disintegrated the moment they'd laid eyes on each other and spoken. She couldn't now walk away and pretend she'd never met the other woman. They were all going to have to be adults and face up to reality.

"My name is Peyton," she said just loud enough for Amelia to hear. The woman froze in place, not turning around but not walking away either. Just standing there as if waiting for Peyton to say more.

"My name is Peyton," she said again, her throat painfully tight. She didn't know if she was doing the right thing or making the worse mistake of her life. "I'm not dead. Not yet, anyway."

Chapter Seven

"CAN I GET you some tea?" Amelia asked, her voice shaking. She stood nervously in the doorway of the kitchen as Ellis and Peyton settled on the sofa in the living room of her home.

Ellis glanced at Peyton but she shook her head. He was proud of how calm she'd acted through all of this mess but his respect for her had soared as he watched how she'd handled herself when meeting Amelia Nelson.

"No, thank you." Ellis grasped Peyton's hand, the skin cold to his touch. "We wanted to speak with you about Greg. Can you do that?"

Amelia nodded and shuttled the children back to their bedrooms, telling them to play for awhile. Wringing her hands together, she sat down in a rocking chair near the fireplace, her face ashen. "Greg told me he was a widower. He showed me a picture of you."

The poor woman was probably working things out in her own head and coming to the conclusion she wasn't legally married to Greg Nelson.

"I'm very much alive," Peyton said softly, sympathy in her eyes for what this other woman was going through. "How did you meet Greg? When did you meet him?"

A small smile curved Amelia's trembling lips. "I met him on the Tube. He was friendly and charming and we went for coffee. That was twelve years ago. We were married about a year later."

Ellis had many questions too but this wasn't his meeting to direct. Peyton needed to take the lead here.

"He must have been gone quite a bit," Peyton said. "What did he tell you?"

"As an artist he traveled doing commissions," Amelia explained. "But he tried to be home as much as possible."

"About half the time?" Peyton asked.

Amelia nodded, releasing a shaky breath. "Yes, that's about right. I guess he wasn't really working. He was with you."

Tugging her hand from Ellis, Peyton clasped them together, the knuckles turning white. "Greg didn't work, not really. He was from a wealthy family. Did he tell you that?"

A few tears were making their way down the woman's face and she shook her head. "No, he said he was an orphan. That he didn't have any family."

Christ, had everything out of that man's mouth been a lie? Had he been truthful ever? Ellis was disgusted by the human being that was Greg Nelson. Peyton deserved a hell of a lot better and frankly, so did this woman and her children.

Peyton cleared her throat. "The remaining money in his trust fund should have gone to you and your children. I'm going to make sure that it does now that I know about you."

Amelia's eyes went wide and she shot up from the chair, pacing the small room. "We're doing fine. Greg left me the insurance policy and he'd purchased this home for us."

That caught Ellis's attention. "Insurance policy?"

Amelia stopped pacing and nodded. "A very generous one. He left us well taken care of."

"I'm not sure you realize just how wealthy Greg's family is," Peyton said carefully, watching the woman's reaction. "They belong to Evandria."

It was a gambit, throwing that out there but Ellis was of the opinion that nothing ventured was nothing gained. If Greg had told Amelia anything about Evandria or Arsenal, they needed to know.

"Evandria?" Amelia frowned in confusion. "That's the insurance company. Do they own it?"

Peyton started next to him and he placed his hand on her knee in what he hoped was a soothing gesture. "The insurance company that paid you was Evandria?"

Nodding, she walked over to a small desk in the corner and sifted through the bottom drawer.

"Yes, I think I still have the paperwork somewhere. I was shocked when they showed up at the door with the check. I had no idea Greg had purchased the policy but I was grateful because it's made things so much easier. Here it is. At the bottom, of course."

Holding out the papers, Ellis reached for them since Peyton hadn't. A cursory examination showed what looked like a life policy from Evandria but he was pretty damn sure that something like this didn't exist.

Peyton took the papers from him and paged through them.

"I'm glad that Greg had the foresight to take out this policy, especially as he had children."

Amelia grabbed the mantle to steady herself. "Do you–Do you have children also?"

Shaking her head, Peyton mustered a smile. "No, I don't."

Classy to the bone, she didn't mention that Greg hadn't wanted any and made her promise not to have them. There was no sense in making this woman wonder if her husband had wanted their children. Leave her with some good memories.

"Oh, I'm sorry," Amelia apologized, her gaze on the fireplace. "I don't really know what to say. This is rather awkward, isn't it?"

"It is," Peyton agreed. "I'm not really sure what to say either."

Sinking back down into the chair, the other woman brushed a stray tear from her cheek.

"I sometimes wondered if he was having an affair. Now I know that I was the other woman."

Peyton was already shaking her head. "No, I don't think of you that way. Greg was...well...he was a man that cared for himself, first and foremost. Don't let his failings make you think less of yourself. I've been there and I won't go back again. This entire situation is because Greg was a selfish, self-centered man."

"I never saw that side of him but I see it now."

"And I'm sorry for that. After seeing you in the park, I'd already decided not to approach you but then your son almost crashed his bike and there we all were."

Picking at the hem of her shirt, Amelia nodded. "I'm actually glad to speak with you. Believe it or not, it helps with the closure. My marriage to Greg was a happy one but I always felt there was something missing. Now I know what it was. Commitment. This makes it easier to move on."

Peyton seemed to have run out of questions so Ellis stepped in. "When Greg died, didn't you wonder about funeral arrangements and so forth? As far as you knew, you were the widow."

"The men from Evandria said that Greg had prearranged everything right down to the cremation. He didn't want a service as he had no family."

A creepy thought occurred to Ellis and it turned his stomach. Who the fuck had Greg's ashes?

He couldn't stop his gaze from traveling to the mantle and Amelia's followed.

Amelia's mouth trembled and more tears threaten to fall. "He wanted his ashes spread over the hills of Ireland. We took a family trip there so I could do that."

Peyton had stiffened next to him and he had the eerie feeling that she had also spread Greg's ashes somewhere. Son of a bitch. This was too cruel to do to anyone.

"I'm sorry that you got caught up in Greg's lies," Peyton sighed. "There were so many."

Was she planning on telling Amelia about Arsenal and Greg's death not being an accident? There didn't seem to be much reason to bring her into this clusterfuck but perhaps she knew more than she was letting on. Maybe Greg had said something that she thought was innocent but they would know its significance.

Amelia straightened and took a deep breath, a smile coming to her face, as the sound of the front door opening reached them.

"I can't be sorry. If I hadn't met Greg I wouldn't have my children, and in a way, he brought my boyfriend into my life as well. When I met him he was working for Evandria. Here he is."

"Hey, sweetheart," a voice called from the foyer. "Did you and the kids have fun at the park?"

That voice. It was familiar to him. To Peyton too, because she was out of her seat and striding toward it with purpose.

A tall, male figure walked into the living room, grinning until he saw that his girlfriend had visitors. Taking a few steps back, his gaze darted from Amelia to Ellis to Peyton as the blood drained from his face.

"Jensen," Peyton hissed, her blue eyes glittering with fury. Her hand had furled into a fist and Ellis knew it was only supreme control that kept her from punching her lying brother in the face. "I think we need to talk. Alone."

Right after Ellis kicked Jensen's ass.

PEYTON DRAGGED HER brother into the foyer, rage bubbling inside of her and bile rising in her throat. He'd known.

"You have one minute to explain yourself." Her jaw ached from gritting her teeth but it was that or smack Jensen. She'd never hit him before but today she might make an exception.

Face pale, Jensen held his hands up in a sign of surrender. "I can explain but please keep your voice down. Amelia doesn't know about any of this."

Mind reeling, she tried to make sense of what she'd learned today. She pressed a hand to her forehead and fought back the tears of betrayal. She'd thought her relationship with Jensen was better than this.

"Another person you supposedly care about but have been lying to?"

Sarcasm dripped from her tone and she didn't give a shit. She was tired of finding out what liars everyone around her was. These days the only people she could depend on were her new friends. And Ellis. Especially Ellis.

As if by magic he appeared in the entryway. "I think she's beginning to figure it out based on our reactions to seeing you, Jensen. You might want to go talk to your girlfriend. She's pretty upset right now."

Brushing past her, Jensen hurried into the living room leaving Ellis and Peyton behind. Her knees wanted to buckle underneath her and for once in her life she didn't hesitate or ponder too long. Instead, she went right to Ellis and leaned against him, needing his strength desperately. His arms went around her and she laid her head on his chest, feeling his steady heartbeat under her ear.

"This is a nightmare," she whispered. "He knew all along. My family is a joke."

"I'd like to argue that."

"But you can't," Peyton finished for him. "I don't think an explanation exists that can make this okay."

His roughened hands were gentle as he ran them up and down her spine in a motion meant to soothe. "No, there isn't but remember you get to choose how you react to all of this, princess. You're in control."

"It doesn't feel like it. It feels like Evandria is just playing with us like a cat with a mouse before he shreds it with his claws."

Ellis lifted her chin so she was looking into his eyes. "Don't give them any more power."

"Actually I feel more powerful since finding out Greg's secrets. It was before that I felt powerless. I don't know if that makes any sense."

"It doesn't have to." He glanced over his shoulder into the living room. "How about we go for a walk, maybe get something to eat, while those two love birds talk. I don't think that's a conversation that's going to move quickly."

She was too angry to eat but she was also too mad to speak to her brother. Thinking straight was a requirement these days and she didn't have the luxury of being scatterbrained when questioning Jensen. Obviously he knew more – much more – than he'd let on.

"Can you tell him we're leaving? If I go in there I'll do something I regret."

Ellis let his arms drop from around her as he stepped back, and she immediately felt the loss of his warmth and strength. He didn't have to say a word, just having him there was more than enough.

"I'll tell him but I want to kick his ass too."

He was going to have to wait in line.

Chapter Eight

PEYTON'S APPETITE WAS better than she'd thought. She had eaten most of her spaghetti Bolognese along with a glass and a half of wine that had mellowed her mood. No longer angry, now she was simply sad. Once more, everything she thought was true turned out to be a lie. This was becoming a bad habit.

"It's okay to be angry," Ellis prompted. "You deserve to be furious. He'll ask for you to forgive him but you don't have to."

She'd thought about that but had come to few conclusions. "Forgiveness isn't possible at the moment, but maybe sometime in the future. Nothing he can say makes this alright. But we both know he's going to give us some babble about Evandria's mission and how it's bigger than the individual. We've heard it all before just from other people."

Ellis checked his phone. "Are you ready to hear him out? I told him where we were and he said he can be here in a few minutes to talk. I can tell him you're not ready if you want me to."

She shook her head. "No, I don't want to drag this out. I'll hear what he has to say and get it over with."

"You're a hell of a lot nicer than I would be under these circumstances."

The image of Ellis dealing with dishonest family members almost brought a smile to her face. He didn't even have patience to deal with bad drivers.

"I'm angered out. I'm tired of being pissed off. I've been in such a heightened state of emotion for so long I can't keep up that sort of intensity forever." But it was more than that and it was time she admitted to it. "The fact is I'm not angry at Greg anymore. I'd have to care to be that mad and I don't. It sounds cold but any love I had for him, he'd killed long before he died. I cared about him as a person all these years but recent events have left me cold. Nothing I do will change what happened in the past nor how Greg handled it. He's not my husband anymore and when I see what he built with Amelia I doubt he ever really was. He was the man that my father wanted me to marry. His family wanted him to marry me too. We were a means to an end. It's hard to stay furious at someone when it feels like they're part of another life."

His brows went up and he opened his mouth to speak but no words came out. She'd apparently rendered him speechless.

I'll write this day down in my calendar.

"What's wrong?" she asked, watching his expression close up and his gaze drop down to his empty plate.

"It's nothing. We should talk about what questions you want to ask Jensen."

Ellis was a cool liar when he needed to be but after spending so much time with him she could see when he was bothered by something. "It's something. Talk to me."

He looked up, his blue eyes almost black with emotion. "If you don't love him anymore, then why...?"

His voice trailed off but he didn't need to finish the sentence for her to know what he was talking about. The elephant in the room that she'd been avoiding since she'd woken up.

Them. Him.

"When you aren't sure about your past, it's hard to plan your future."

His gaze scrutinized her so closely she wanted to crawl under the table and hide. Ellis saw everything, and he wouldn't let her hide from the truth.

"I would imagine it would be even harder to avoid it." He leaned forward and captured her hand with his, their fingers tangling together. No other man's touch had ever felt so good and right, the tingling running up her arm and straight to her abdomen. "Your future is happening as we speak, princess. If you don't want me, that's fine. I'm a big boy and I'll survive. But if you're waiting on some sign from the universe, you might be waiting for awhile. In the meantime, your life is passing you by and I can assure you with absolutely no doubt in my mind that tomorrow isn't a guarantee."

It had come down to this. They'd been dancing around this topic for days now, the awareness between them growing stronger with each passing moment. She'd hoped to dodge this conversation for a little longer, knowing she'd have to tell him the truth. He deserved no less and she wouldn't disrespect all his sacrifice with a lie.

It was there on the tip of her tongue, the words she needed to say but that she didn't want him to hear. Time seemed to stand still as he waited for her reply, giving her no quarter to evade him. Endless patience, that's what Ellis Hunter had. How many suspects had he broken under this interrogation technique? Too many to count. He was a professional and she was an amateur when it came to subterfuge. The only person that had ever believed her lies was herself, and she'd fallen hook, line, and sinker.

"I'm scared."

Her voice sounded rusty and unused but that was simply the lump that had grown in her throat as she'd contemplated her few options. Lies and truth. Truth and lies. She couldn't tell even the smallest fib to this man, but that's what made him different than anyone else she'd ever met.

Her authenticity must have pleased him because he lifted her hand to his lips and pressed a kiss to the knuckles, sending a million butterflies free in her stomach. No one had ever done that to her before and once wasn't going to be enough.

"Can you tell me what you're scared of? Is it me?"

Shaking her head, she sought the right answer in her muddled brain. "No. Yes. Kind of. I'm scared of the way you make me feel."

"How do I make you feel?"

His voice was soft, low, and cajoling as if she was a bird on the windowsill he didn't want to fly away.

She couldn't hold back the first word that came to mind. "Weak."

His mouth went slack and she wished she could take her answer back but it was far too late.

"Weak," he repeated, his features bleak. "I guess I would be afraid too if you made me feel that way."

She had no right to ask but...

"How do I make you feel?"

His gaze raked her up and down, sending a zing of electricity to every molecule in her body. He didn't try and hide the fact that he liked what he saw.

"Happy."

This from the grouchy detective she'd met that first day. The man that never seemed happy about anything was happy because of her.

"That's...good."

He shrugged and signaled the waitress. "Depends on how you look at it. I've never found much usefulness in the emotion but I can't deny how you make me feel."

"It's good to be happy, Ellis."

"Is it? It changes nothing except your mood. It doesn't accomplish anything. Lots of productive people in the world weren't happy. It's not a requirement."

He was defensive now because of what she'd said. "I need to explain what I said—"

"You owe me nothing," he cut in, not letting her finish. "Not a thing. If I make you feel weak, then I do. No explanations necessary. Now let's get ready because your brother just walked into the restaurant."

Jensen was striding across the room, determination written across his face. He'd had time to think about what he wanted to say so she was surely in for an earful of excuses.

She had a few things to say as well.

Chapter Nine

JENSEN WAS FULL of excuses, clearly not wanting to take responsibility for his decisions and actions. Ellis didn't have any respect for people like that.

"I didn't know until after Greg died," Jensen pleaded for his sister's understanding as they sat in a quiet corner of the restaurant. "It didn't seem the right time to tell you."

Peyton's normally sedate blue eyes were full of fire. "It's been five years. Are you trying to say that you couldn't find the balls to tell me the truth for all that time? That's pathetic."

"Now wait a minute," Jensen sputtered, his cheeks turning red. "I was trying to protect you."

Ellis couldn't keep his damn mouth shut. "Get real. You were protecting yourself."

Swinging his attention from his sister, Jensen turning his frustration onto Ellis. "Can you keep out of this? This is a family matter."

The young millionaire had pulled the family card. Predictable.

Peyton didn't give Ellis a moment to reply.

"It became his business the minute he put his life on the line for me." Peyton shook her finger at her brother, clearly incensed. "He's been more loyal than my own family. You've been lying to me for years. What else do I not know about? Am I adopted too? Because that would explain a whole hell of a lot in my life."

Jensen's fingers tightened around the cloth napkin that was sitting on the table. "You are not adopted although I'm sure you wish you were. Sorry, sis, you're one of us. Now will you let me explain?"

"Don't you mean make excuses?" Peyton rolled her eyes. "That's all I've heard from your lips since you got here. Lousy fucking excuses."

"I didn't want to add to your grief. You were even more adrift after Greg died than before. What if I told you and you did something drastic? I couldn't have that on my conscience."

"So this was about you?" she scoffed. "I knew it. I asked our parents and they said they didn't know but I suppose that's a lie too. The question isn't if they know but how long have they known?"

Scraping a hand down his face, Jensen shook his head. "I honestly don't know if they know or knew before. I definitely don't think Mother did. She hates Evandria and doesn't want anything to do with them, but Father might have known at some point. He's been an officer for the organization and he would have had access to the files. He's never said anything to me one way or another. We don't discuss Evandria business but he does go to meetings."

Ellis's ears perked up. "He does? He said he'd never heard of Arsenal but if he was an officer he definitely would have, correct? He had to have known Greg was a member."

Jensen hemmed and hawed, obviously not wanting to impli-
cate his father but it was too late. The senior McMillen was a
total asshole and a shitty parent.

"Probably," he finally admitted with a sigh. "Arsenal isn't
well-known among the membership but to the officers it would
be. As for knowing who is a part of that division, maybe not.
That sort of list wouldn't be common knowledge."

"I didn't think Dad was an officer anymore."

"He's not but as a longtime member and former officer there
are some perks."

Leaning forward, Ellis looked Jensen straight in the eyes. He
wanted a truthful fucking answer. "Are you in Arsenal?"

"No." The other man shook his head and shifted uncomfort-
ably in his chair. "I'm not, I swear."

Ellis didn't let up on Peyton's brother. "Did you help kill
Greg?"

Jensen reared up in indignation. "Hell, no. I liked Greg. He
was a nice guy."

"Then why was your name brought up on a recording between two of the men responsible for his death?"

Hand trembling, Jensen shook his head. "It was some other
Jensen. I swear I don't know them."

"They said that you would take care of me if I wanted to go
to the restaurant that day. Did you know they were going to kill
Greg?"

Tugging at his collar, her brother was clearly agitated. "No!"

Heads turned in the dining room and Jensen lowered his
voice. "No, I didn't have anything to do with it. I don't know
who would have been talking about me."

Ellis really hated Peyton's brother at this moment. "So if you aren't in Arsenal and you weren't part of Greg's murder then why were you tasked with going to see Greg's other wife and giving her some bogus insurance settlement? It kind of sounds like Evandria wanted you to tell Peyton."

Jensen shrugged. "When I was asked I didn't know the whole story. Then after I said yes, it seemed like an innocuous request, they gave me the rest of the details. I did ask them why me, and they said that they thought I would be sensitive to the delicacy of the information. Better to keep it in the family than let someone who wasn't related do it. It seemed like a good idea."

It was a lousy idea and Evandria was playing God again, pushing people around like pawns on a chess board. They had to control every goddamn thing but the weather, and Ellis would wager they were working on that.

"And then you started dating her."

Peyton's tone was bitter and Jensen winced at her words.

"It didn't start out like that. She was so sad and alone and I just wanted to make sure she was okay. I'd come around and visit every now and then. We were friends really, and then it grew into more. I really love her and I want to marry her."

She took a gulp of her wine. "How romantic. Congratulations on your future together. Or is she mad at you too? It didn't sound like she was taking the news very well when we left."

Her brother's throat bobbed and he rubbed the back of his neck. "I think everything is okay now. She says she understands why I didn't tell her."

"Then she understands more than I do," Peyton said bitterly.

"So far you've given the world's worst excuses and it all comes down to you being a pussy and trying to save your own skin. You were the one person in our family that I thought I could trust, and now I know that you've been lying to me and her for years. I don't trust you, I don't respect you, and I'm not even sure I want to be your sister right now. Maybe I'll get over this eventually but your duplicity makes me sick."

Ellis was so fucking proud of the way Peyton stood up for herself he almost applauded. Jensen looked ill, his skin a greenish-gray and his eyes bright with tears. Some might call her statements over the top but it didn't look like Jensen had ever had to deal with the consequences of his actions before. This was a good life lesson.

If you act like a shit, people aren't going to like you very much.

"I can only say I'm sorry," he mumbled, looking down at his hands in his lap. "I've messed up and I don't know how to fix it."

Reaching under the table, Ellis placed his hand on Peyton's thigh, giving it a squeeze to let her know he was there for her no matter what. Some of the tension underneath his palm relaxed away and she sighed, placing her own hand on top of his.

Drained of energy and anger, Peyton appeared to have run out of gas. She slumped in her chair, her lips pressed together and deliberately not looking at her asshole brother. It was time for Ellis to step into the questioning.

"Do you know Grant Hollister? And try to tell the truth this time."

Fidgeting in his chair, Jensen nodded. "I know him. He's considered to be up and coming for an officer position."

"Did you know he was Alex Vaughn's half-brother?"

Jensen's head jerked up. "I didn't. Are you sure?"

"Quite sure. Now tell me what you know of Evandria now that Archer Caldwell has been placed in custody. What's going on as far as a power struggle? Do you know who will take his place? Will it be Nigel Holmwood?"

"Nigel?" He shook his head. "It won't be him. It will probably be one of the current officers but I don't know which one. There'll be an election of the officers and the division heads. There are rumblings that it might be someone outside the power structure but that's just a rumor. It's always the same every time a new president is elected but then an officer gets the position anyway."

Ellis would love to be a fly on the wall during that meeting. "What was Archer Caldwell's position before he was president?"

Silence and then a sigh. "Jesus, I shouldn't be telling you all this."

Swiveling in her chair, Peyton shot him an angry look. "But you will, brother dear, because you owe me. You'll tell the truth for perhaps the first time in your life."

Jensen scratched his head and groaned before answering. "Archer was the division head for Arsenal."

Arsenal. Of course. Caldwell had been lying when he'd said he wasn't aware of Frank, Alex, and Greg's deaths until recently. Another asshole.

"That's the power position, isn't it?" Ellis challenged. "That position feeds into the presidency, doesn't it?"

"Yes."

"What's your title, Jensen? You say you aren't in Arsenal.

What do you do for Evandria? They had you deliver their hush money to Amelia. Are you in the financial division?"

Straightening in his chair, Jensen made a cutting motion with his hand. "It wasn't hush money. Evandria knew that Greg hadn't made any provisions for her and they wanted to make it right. He was one of us and we take care of our own."

"They sure do," Ellis scoffed. "They took care of those three men and made sure they aren't looking at the green side of the grass. Lovely people you socialize with. Now what's your title?"

"I'm an assistant to the director of the financial division."

"Are you next in line to be director?" Peyton asked.

"Yes. Probably."

Ellis smiled, already knowing the answer to the question he was about to ask. "When did you receive this title? Assistant to the director of whatever."

Jensen's shoulders sagged and he slumped down. "After I handled the payout to Amelia for Greg's death."

"Bastard," Peyton spat, her muscles rigid under his fingers. "You're just like all the rest of them. It's all about the power."

That brought up another question. "Which side of the power struggle was Caldwell on? The good or the bad? And don't pretend you don't know what I'm talking about because you do."

"The rogue," Jensen replied after a long pause.

Hell, I might as well swing for the fences.

"Holmwood?"

"The good. I think. I'm not really sure."

"Greg?"

Jensen shook his head. "I don't know."

"Your father?"

"I don't know."

"Grant Hollister?"

"I don't know," he replied, sweat running down his forehead. "I don't know. We don't know things like that."

Ellis leaned forward, his fingers tightening on Peyton's. "Just one more question and this one you should know the answer to quite easily. Which side are you on, Jensen?"

Eyes red-rimmed, the man blinked rapidly to hold back the tears as his lips trembled. A sob erupted from his throat and he scrubbed at his face with the back of his hand.

"I don't know. I truly have no idea."

Peyton threw down her napkin in disgust. "I'm going to the ladies' room."

Normally Ellis wouldn't let her go by herself but the restroom was only a few feet away. He didn't object as she disappeared behind the door, glad to have a few minutes to chat with Jensen who was dabbing at his eyes with his napkin.

For fuck's sake. Nut up, man.

Clearing his throat to get Jensen's attention, Ellis leaned closer so he didn't have to raise his voice. "I'm glad we have a chance to talk. You know, man to man."

Jensen sniffled and nodded. "I'm glad that Peyton has someone like you to keep an eye on her."

Ellis kept his voice low. "That's exactly what I intend to do. If you or your Evandria friends have any ideas about hurting her, I will hunt you down like the dogs you are and make it look like an accident. They'll never find the body. Do you get what I'm saying?"

The other man had shrunk away from Ellis, horror written on his face. "I–No–Jesus–"

Ellis didn't hesitate to make sure his point was clear as a bell. There would be no misunderstandings after this. "Jesus won't be able to help you, Jensen. Hear me well. If Peyton or her friends get so much as a fucking hangnail, I will make your fucking nightmares look like a fucking paradise. It will be my mission in life to make you and your friends so fucking miserable you'll be begging me on your knees for death. I hope we understand each other because it appears that no one on this stupid planet has ever put that woman first. That's all changed now. She's the most important thing in my life. You? I really don't give a shit if you live or die. I could go either way on that so don't test me. You'll lose." Ellis picked up his wine glass and took a sip. "I'm so glad we had this talk. I, for one, feel so much better. How about you?"

His eyes wide and unblinking, Jensen nodded but didn't say a word. Just as well. Ellis didn't believe a word coming out of the man's mouth.

Trust no one.

Chapter Ten

PEYTON STARED AT the ceiling of her hotel bedroom, wide awake despite the late hour. She could blame the time difference but inside she knew better. She'd hurt Ellis – the last person in the world she'd wanted to injure – earlier today when she'd told him he made her weak. He didn't understand what she'd meant and he hadn't wanted to give her a chance to explain it better. She wasn't even sure that she could, only that she had to try.

Tossing back the covers, she grabbed her robe from the end of the bed, wrapping it around her chilled body. It was much cooler in London than she was used to and she didn't forget to slide her feet into slippers before padding out of the bedroom into the living area of the suite they'd rented. She already knew from her time in the hospital that Ellis only slept a few hours a night and with any luck he'd be awake as well.

The television was the only light, casting shadows across the empty sofa bed where he should have been. For a moment her heart skipped a beat, thinking that he might have left her but reason kicked in immediately. This was Ellis Hunter and he didn't leave a job undone.

Sweeping the room, her gaze landed on his dark figure leaning against the balcony sliding doors, a highball glass in his hand. He hadn't even undressed for bed, still clad in his blue jeans and white button-down shirt. The sleeves were rolled up to his elbows revealing muscular forearms with just a sprinkling of dark hair covering his golden skin. Ellis was a handsome man although he was even more devastating on the rare occasions he smiled. It transformed his entire face and made her want to trace the crinkles around his eyes with her fingertips.

She wasn't going to do any of that. Tonight she was going to attempt to explain how her issues didn't have anything to do with him and everything to do with her. He was wonderful she was...messed up.

Instead of going to stand next to him, she walked over to the bar in the corner of the room and poured herself a generous whiskey. She'd been avoiding alcohol in case she needed to take any medication but if she ever needed a drink, it was right now. Carrying her glass in one hand and the bottle in the other, she came up right behind him, close enough to feel the warmth radiate from his body but far enough away that she could keep her sanity.

Holding out the bottle, she said, "Refill?"

He didn't turn, seemingly content to stare out on the London skyline but he held his glass out to the side. "Don't mind if I do."

She refilled his glass and walked back to the bar to replace the whiskey on the counter. The tension in the room had begun to build and was becoming unbearable. Part of her wanted him to say something, anything, and a bigger part of her was terrified of what he might say. Would he rail against her and call her a tease? Would he tell her she was spoiled and selfish, dragging him here when she had no intention of the relationship being anything other than business? Would he decide she wasn't worth the hassle and leave her once he'd delivered her back to the States?

She wouldn't blame him for any of that but deep down she knew none of that was going to happen. Men like Ellis, old school to the core, didn't turn their anger on a woman. They internalized it until they dropped dead from a heart attack at fifty. That's what she'd be to him someday. A heart condition.

She couldn't take his cold indifference a moment longer. "Are you going to look at me?"

"Why? Do you look different?"

Nobody could be a grumpy asshole better than Ellis. He'd dropped most of his bullshit with her but tonight that wall was in full force.

"Don't be a jerk."

She heard him chuckle in the dark but his back was still facing her. "But I am a jerk, princess."

Sometimes, but not all the time, and never to her.

"Are you drunk?

She didn't know how she knew, but she could *feel* him smiling. He found her amusing, like a cat playing with a mouse.

"Not even close. I have to keep my wits sharp to keep you alive. Did you know I threatened to kill your brother today when you were in the ladies' room? He almost shit his pants he was so scared. From what I've observed so far, the wealthy don't seem to have much balls."

Jensen didn't. It also explained why her brother had barely said two words when she'd returned to the table.

"You were angry at me so you took it out on Jensen?"

"I took it out on Jensen because he's a fucking waste of oxygen. As for anger, I'm not mad at you."

"You are."

He took a sip of his whiskey, the amber liquid catching a shaft of light from a building across the street. "I'm really not. You feel how you feel. It would be a waste of energy to be upset about that."

She took a gulp from her own drink and choked on the fire as the flames burned the back of her throat. "And you don't waste energy."

"I don't waste. Period. Is that what you got out of bed for? A drink and a philosophy lesson?"

The air around her seemed permeated with his masculine scent, spicy and warm. It reminded her of hot summer nights at the beach, the smell of salt in the air and the heavy perfume of citrus and hibiscus. Ellis was the moon in a starless night sky, pulling at her like the tide until she was helpless, without a will of her own. Her senses were completely attuned to his every breath, every eyelash flicker, every twitch of his fingers.

She'd imagined those hands on her skin, fantasized about what they could do to her. He'd touched her before of course in the most casual of ways. His hands had been rough, just enough to cause a friction against her much softer flesh. They were a man's hands, hard, unrelenting, and capable of bodily harm. But this was a man also capable of great tenderness. He'd soothed her headaches with cold compresses on her forehead, rubbed her shoulders after a nightmare, and read to her when she couldn't sleep.

Ellis Hunter was a man of contradictions, every one of them fascinating, compelling, and exciting. Was it any wonder that he made her feel weak? It was only earlier tonight when he'd challenged her feelings toward him that she'd admitted to the emotions she'd been so carefully trying to ignore. If she pretended they weren't there, perhaps they might simply disappear.

Life didn't work that way.

"I came out here to talk to you." Her voice sounded gravelly as if it hadn't been used in a long time.

"I'm listening."

Sighing, she reached out and placed her hand on his arm, feeling the muscles flinch under her touch. "Will you turn around?"

For a moment she thought he would refuse but then he did, unhurried as if they had all night. His eyes were hooded, his lips a straight line. They were back to the beginning when Ellis kept his emotions under careful check. She'd undone weeks of work with one word.

"What did you want to talk about, princess?"

There was still time to turn and run back into the bedroom, locking the door behind her and not coming out until morning. He wouldn't chase her, that was for sure. He didn't want to have this conversation any more than she did; hell, probably much less actually. He'd let it all go and tomorrow morning pretend this had never happened. All she had to do was turn around and walk away.

Her heart beating like thunder in her ears, she stood her ground. For once in her life, she needed to be brave. He'd called her a fierce warrior and she wanted to believe she really could be. That had been one of her resolutions when she'd woken up in that hospital, scared and disoriented. Of course it had been easy to think that when Ellis had been by her side the entire time. His face was the first thing she'd seen when she'd opened her eyes.

"What I meant when I said that you made me weak—it's not what you think."

His lips curved into a smile but she knew he wasn't happy. He had been but he wasn't now. "And what do I think?"

She'd built this. This mocking, sarcastic man was her fault.

"You think I meant it in a bad way. But that's not the case."

"Because being weak is such a good thing."

There was derision in his tone but she could hear the hurt as well.

"You do make me feel weak," she admitted. "But not in a bad way. Maybe a better way to describe it is that you *allow* me to feel weak. I trust you enough that I don't always have to be the one in charge, in control all the time. Greg was like a child that needed his mommy and I had to be the grownup. I don't feel that way with you. I can allow myself to just be. It's a luxury I'm not used to."

The silence stretched out as he pondered her explanation. She wanted to rush in and explain more, find the right words, but Ellis didn't need more from her. Finally he straightened and took another sip of his whiskey.

"But you don't like it."

He didn't phrase it like a question.

Swallowing hard, she nodded. "It unnerves me. I don't know how to feel this way and it scares me. You scare me."

She heard his swiftly drawn breath. "I scare you?"

"Not in that way. You scare me in that I don't know what to do. I don't know how to handle feeling this vulnerable. How am I supposed to deal with this?"

His brow quirked. "Enjoy it? Isn't it nice to not have to be in charge of every fucking thing, every fucking minute of the day?"

This was rich coming from him. "I don't know and you don't either. Pot? This is kettle. You're just as guilty as I am, Ellis."

"You're wrong." He shook his head and walked over to the bar but he didn't refill his glass. "As a cop, I know when to depend on other people. Everyone has a role to play, and everyone can't be in charge. It doesn't work that way. I'm in charge right now because I'm trying to keep you alive. Next time we go shopping, princess, it's all you. I'll happily walk behind you and carry your handbag."

Chauvinist asshole.

"I hate to shop," she said, stalling for time. She hadn't thought about his job in those terms, but it didn't change the panic she'd been feeling. "I can't lose myself in you, Ellis. I've lived too much of my life like that."

"I don't remember asking you to do that. Peyton, if I wanted someone to follow me around and worship me I'd get a fucking puppy from Josh. I'm looking for a partner in my life, someone who can handle me. Give as good as they get. Someone who takes no shit from me. I'm not sure where you think you haven't done exactly that. You're a strong woman."

Am I?

"This is why I'm keeping my distance. I'm so confused right now. Ellis, I need time. That's all I'm asking for. A little time. Can you give me that?"

"I'd give you the goddamn moon if you asked me for it." He slammed his glass down on the bar and strode up to her, his large hands on her shoulders so she had to look up at him. "I'll give you all the time that you want but I'm going to need something for myself."

She nodded numbly, not trusting her voice when he was this close. Every cell in her body was screaming out to press herself into his arms but her head... It was shouting warnings as if she was going down on the *Titanic*.

"I need to take a few steps back." Her world tilted at the thought he wanted to leave her and he must have seen her panic because he was shaking his head. "Not physically. I'm in this and I won't leave you. I told you I'll protect you with my life and I meant it. But emotionally I need some space as well. I respect that you need time and I want to give you that, but to do it I need to disengage a little for my own sanity."

She couldn't say no. He'd risked his life for her and had never asked for one little thing. Until now. This was because she'd pushed him to it. This was a reaction to her.

"Yes, I can do that."

"And I can give you all the time you need."

His hands fell away from her arms and she wanted to beg him to put them back. Already she could feel his emotional withdrawal even if he hadn't take one step away from her. The room felt colder and she wrapped her arms around herself to ward off the chill.

"Then we understand each other."

The words sounded hollow and trite and she cringed at herself. This whole conversation had gone to hell. It might have been better to have said nothing at all.

"We do," he agreed, throwing back the last of his drink. "I'm still here for you. That hasn't changed. I just can't keep putting myself out there for you if there isn't any hope for me. For us. It's not your fault, it's just the way I am."

She wanted to yell that there was hope but the fear took over and she said nothing. Truthfully, she didn't know if she could ever give him what he was seeking. It all sounded so wonderful, a real partnership with a loving man that respected her. It was all she'd ever wanted. But she needed to be strong, and stand on her own two feet. She'd lived in someone's shadow too long.

Turning and walking back to her room, she already missed Ellis. His smile, his laugh, his keen intellect, and even his grumpy demeanor before his coffee.

If this was what being strong felt like, maybe it wasn't what she wanted to be.

Chapter Eleven

AWKWARD AND COLD. That's how Peyton would describe her relationship with Ellis after their conversation last night. She was awkward and he was cold. Now that she'd pushed him away, she didn't know what to say or do. All the friendly, warm actions that she'd come to depend on from him were gone.

Normally he'd be up first in the morning, have the coffee made and the newspaper spread out over the table. She'd read aloud to him from the articles while they ate breakfast. It had been a silly thing she'd done her first day out of the hospital after the nurses told her that Ellis had read to her every day while she was in a coma.

Today, the coffee had been made but there had been no smiling greeting. There was no chatting as she picked at her eggs and toast. They orbited around one another in the suite as he read his emails and she pretended to read the headlines. He wasn't being cruel or nasty. He was simply being professional.

She hated it, but she'd brought it on herself.

Ellis folded the newspaper. "We need to go out and get another burner phone and maybe even change hotels. I'm getting that feeling again. Yesterday I felt like someone was watching us but keeping their distance."

His cop's instincts. He'd kept her alive this long so she wouldn't argue with them now.

"I'm tired. Do you mind if I stay behind here in the room? I can look for a new place to stay while you get new phones."

He gazed at her sharply, his eyes narrowed suspiciously. "I don't want you out of my sight."

She hadn't been for days but after last night, she simply needed an hour to herself. She couldn't begin to gather her thoughts about this man when he was right next to her. He had a way of muddling her thinking and making her want to curl up in his lap, closing out the cruel world around them.

"I'll stay here," she pressed. "I won't open the door for anybody. Wouldn't I be safer here than out on the street?"

Stroking his chin, he pondered her plea. As smart as he was, he had to know this wasn't because she was tired. This had everything to do with them.

"I don't know—"

"You said it yourself. Anyone could get to me out there." She pointed to the windows, the sun shining brightly outside this morning. "Surely the room is the safest place for me?"

He shook his head, a muscle ticking in his jaw. "And anyone could get you in here. The lock on that door isn't solid steel. One good swift kick and it would fall apart. You're vulnerable wherever we go, but at least if I'm with you I can watch for threats. No, you come with me."

"But—"

"Goddamit, Peyton, will you listen to me?" he growled, hopping up from the chair. "I'm trying to keep you alive but if you don't give a shit, I'll catch the next flight back to the States while you visit Buckingham Palace and have tea with the Queen."

That was his frustration and hurt talking so she didn't rise to the bait. Her fingers curled around the edge of the table and she took another scalding sip of her coffee before replying.

"I do give a shit," she said quietly. "I was just—"

"Trying to fucking avoid being in my company," he stated, ice dripping in his tone. "I know. I'm a grouchy ass detective with bad table manners. Got it. Now get your fanny out of that chair and get ready to go. When we get back, we need to decide what we're going to do next. If Jensen or your parents aren't going to tell us anything more it might be best if we just went back home."

Her home or his home? Separately or together? She didn't take offense at what he'd said. She'd been around him long enough to know when he was hitting out at others like a bear with a sore paw. He was also worried as hell. His shoulders were rigid and his gaze was constantly darting around, looking for anyone that wanted to hurt her. The only place he even slightly relaxed was inside the suite. The immense stress he was under had to be taking its toll but he never complained about the lack of sleep or the incredible responsibility.

Retrieving her purse, she followed Ellis out of the hotel, neither of them saying a word. It was a relief to be outside and doing something, even if it wasn't a fun or pleasant errand. Craning her neck to look up into Ellis's face, all she found was the scowl she'd first seen when they'd met. It was his default expression with most people.

"Maybe we should call the others when we get back to the room? Find out if anything has changed at home," she suggested, trying to break the chilly ice that had settled between them. All her instincts were urging her to reach out and take his hand but his remote demeanor had her keeping her distance.

"That's fine."

No, everything wasn't fine. She'd screwed it up.

They couldn't even talk to each other anymore. This was a man that knew some of her more humiliating secrets and she couldn't find the words to make everything okay. She'd meant to push him away and she'd succeeded beyond her wildest dreams. What had she thought he would do? Smile and continue being wonderful when she'd given him an emotional smackdown? Maybe Bailey and Willow were right. She did live in a little optimistic fantasy world.

His arm went around her waist and curled tightly around her arm, but he stayed facing forward. "Listen to me closely, princess. Do not look over your shoulder, but I think we're being followed."

Her pulse kicked into high gear as adrenaline flooded her veins. He hadn't been short with her because he was mad. He'd been watching to keep her alive.

It took every ounce of willpower not to turn her head and look. She wanted to see what he saw but then he hadn't turned around either. This was all instinct. "What do we do?"

The sidewalk was crowded as they continued down the street. Her skin crawled as she could physically feel eyes on her back. She'd thought she'd become used to the idea of being watched.

Guess not.

"I'm deciding that now. We have a few options, each one worse than the last. We could try and catch a taxi and hope we get lost in the traffic. We could get to the nearest Tube station and catch the next train to anywhere. We could go into one of those shops and hope they have a back door into an alleyway. We can keep walking and try and shake them."

He was right, none of them were ideal.

"I trust you."

For a moment she thought his steps had faltered but he'd simply pushed them forward, trying to get her walk faster. They were moving quickly down the sidewalk now and she'd broken out into a sweat, whether from fear or exertion she didn't know. Maybe both.

"Do you?" he asked, his voice tight. "Because they're gaining on us. I can feel them behind me. I think there are two of them. I hope, anyway. Two I can take. Three or more and I just might get my ass kicked."

She didn't know what he was talking about but he continued speaking as if she did. "This is how we're going to play this, Peyton. We're going to dart in and out of these shops. I don't think they'll try anything when there are a lot of people around. But if we get separated for any reason, we need a meeting spot. Where is that place you're always talking about?"

"The Tate Modern, and I'm not leaving you."

She could see the corner of his mouth turn up. "I could have sworn not twenty minutes ago you were anxious to ditch me.

Here's your chance."

She hadn't been thinking straight. "What happened to I'm safer with you?"

"Normally I would stand behind those words but I can't guarantee that you and I can stay together. Let's see if we can shake them. If we can't, we'll get in the first taxi we can find and get the hell out of here. You have your passport, right? We can't go back to the room."

She did. He'd always preached that she should be ready to abandon the hotel at any moment. It looked like she was going to lose her favorite red cotton sweater.

"What if they follow us in another taxi?"

"I didn't say it was a perfect plan. I need to call the others and then find a place to lie low until I figure out our next move." His tone was soft but urgent as his fingers flew over the face of his phone. "Remember what I said. If anything happens to me, you find someplace to hide for a day or two, wait for the others. Have them come get you. Do you understand?"

She did and she didn't like it in the least. "I'm not going anywhere without you."

They were stopped at the crosswalk, waiting for the light to turn. "You will do what you need to do to survive. If they hurt me or kill me, you need to run. Far and fast. I can't help you if I'm incapacitated so don't hang around to assess the damage."

"You're a grouchy old bastard," she muttered under her breath as they crossed the street.

"And then some," he agreed. "They're even closer now. It feels different this time. Normally they just hang back and watch. They're stalking us like prey, making us walk in circles, trying to confuse me. Let's go into that bakery."

The prickles on her neck were growing in intensity. Her own heart was beating so loudly it was amazing that all of London couldn't hear her. The smell of freshly baked bread permeated the air as they crossed the threshold into the shop crammed full of people.

"This way," he said suddenly, grabbing her arm and dragging her around the counter. The employees were so busy with the crowd they didn't even notice two people heading into the backroom. "Don't say anything while we walk through here. With luck they won't notice us."

Her mind whirred and she nodded. She kept her head down as they walked by the hot ovens and out of the door that had been propped open to let in a cool breeze. Quickly they shot down the alley and into the back door of another shop. This back area appeared to be a storage room but luckily no one was in it as they hurried through another door to what she hoped was the main area.

They almost smacked into a young woman when they opened the door and she whirled around, hands on her hips, an unhappy expression on her face.

"What were you doing back there? That's for employees on-ly."

Ellis shot her his most charming smile. "Sorry. Lost Americans. Lovely country."

They were out the front entrance and back on the street before she could reply. Half running now, they crossed the street and headed up the block.

"Did we lose them?"

"I think they split up and one of them is behind us. We need to try another tactic. Are you ready?"

Probably not, but it didn't matter anyway. Her answer was lost in the wind as he opened the door to an idling taxi and shoved her inside, tossing a stack of money at the driver and shouting at him to go. *Now.* The driver's mouth hung open but he seemed to get the message, revving the engine and tearing away from the curb.

The cab driver turned sharply and she fell against Ellis, her stomach heaving in her abdomen and her body trembling all over.

"The Eye," Ellis grunted, twisting in his seat so he could see out of the back window.

"Did we shake them now?"

He turned back, his shoulders rising and falling with each breath. "I think so but just in case we'll take this cab to The Eye and then switch to a new one. Looks like we can't go back to the hotel and I think staying in London is also a huge no. I think we need to get to the station and take the first train out of the city." He looked at her strangely. "Peyton, are you listening to me?"

She nodded numbly, barely able to speak. "Yes."

"I won't let anything happen to you."

"I know."

The thought of what could have happened back there had slapped her sideways, grabbing her complete attention.

As the taxi sped through traffic, the enormity of what had almost happened hit her like she was running into a brick wall at a hundred miles an hour. Evandria had escalated and were now actively seeking them. Wanting them dead. A wave of nausea came over her and she had to fight to keep her breakfast down, her hand pressed against her stomach.

They were sitting ducks and Evandria's men were the hunters.

Time to disappear.

Chapter Twelve

T HE TRAIN RIDE to Oxford took less than an hour and a half. Ellis and Peyton had left everything behind so they were going to have to replace all their clothes and toiletries and then find a place to stay for the night.

He'd given all of his cash to that cabbie to get him to drive like a maniac and break a few traffic laws.

He'd be upset if he and his friends hadn't thought ahead. Both Josh and Chase owned corporations and they'd each given him a corporate credit card in case they needed a large expenditure but didn't want to use their names. Evandria probably knew about their company names but it wouldn't be the first listing they'd look under. It might slow them down. A little.

Once he found them a place to stay, he and Peyton could sit tight for a day or two until he, Chase, and Josh decided their next move. His vote was to return to America. He felt more in control of the situation there, although he didn't know why. It was just as dangerous in the States as in London. At least if he was in Williamsburg, he'd know the local cops and have backup when things got messy like today.

It was too bad he and Peyton weren't in Oxford on vacation. It was a lovely place and the people seemed friendly, although Ellis had already coached her not to chat too much with anyone. The one thing he didn't want them to do was make any sort of impression on the locals. It would be hard for a woman who looked like Peyton to fade into the background but they needed to try. If Evandria's goons came asking about them, Ellis wanted the people to be able to honestly say they hadn't seen them.

"First things first," he said, that feeling of being watched no longer present. For now, at least, they had some breathing room. "We need new burner phones and we need clothes and tooth-brushes."

He wasn't sure he liked the way Peyton looked at him as if he had two heads and three nostrils. Did she think they should be doing something else?

"How can you be like this?"

"Like what?"

She motioned around them. "Like…this. One minute we're close to being annihilated by a secret society and the next we're picking out underwear. That was probably the single scariest moment of my life back there. They wanted us."

He nodded, careful not to feed into her fears. She needed him to be calm and strong right now. "They did, but they didn't get us. They won't get us if I have anything to say about it. As for how I do it, I just try not to think about it."

Cocking her head to the side, she rubbed her temple. He needed to make sure she didn't overdo. She wasn't long out of the hospital. "That's the big detective secret? Just don't think about it. Words of wisdom."

"Everything isn't a sonnet, princess. Now let's buy you some panties. Hell, that may be the first time in my life I've said those words."

They didn't get far before Ellis's phone buzzed and he checked his texts. Chase and Josh were all over the situation as he'd known they would be. He stopped on the corner and moved out of the way of foot traffic, keeping Peyton at his side.

"Josh, talk to me."

"Are you there?" his friend asked. "We got you a place to stay centrally located about a ten minute walk from the station. According to the website, there are lots of shops and restaurants close by. The reservation is under my corporate account. I texted you the information."

One item checked off the list.

"That sounds great. Hopefully this will be the last call on this phone and we'll be on a new one here within the hour. What about you?"

"We're moving to the next on the list."

Ellis had given his friends several burners and he had the list of numbers in his pocket.

"Good move. We can't be too careful, especially after this morning."

"Do you really think they were trying to kidnap Peyton? Maybe you too?"

He was convinced of it. They'd been too close for anything else.

"I do," he said firmly. "They're raising the stakes since Caldwell was caught and now she's talked to her brother and father. I think we can safely say that they didn't like that at all."

Peyton elbowed him in the ribs. She didn't like it when he talked about her as if she wasn't standing right next to him.

"I'll call you when we get settled into our room. Then we need to discuss the next steps."

"We can come get you. Willow said she can have the jet gassed up and be there in no time."

Ellis had thought about that but it seemed more dangerous to have the four of them traveling. He wouldn't put it past Evandria to take down an airplane. If they hadn't already. Everything that had happened in the past was now suspect.

"I think we should lie low for a few days. See if they try again."

"Whatever you think. We can talk about it later. Anything else we can do for you?"

"Nothing. We'll talk tonight."

He hung up and turned back to Peyton who had been waiting patiently. Sort of.

"Are you ready to go shopping? It's on Chase today."

Wrinkling her nose at him, she nodded her head. "How many days am I shopping for?"

"I don't know. Let's start with two and go from there."

And no more. He wanted to get them home as soon as humanly possible.

It was back to awkward. While they'd been on the run, Ellis had – mostly – reverted to the man she'd become close to these past weeks. Always intense, he'd gone into overdrive getting them out of London but he'd succeeded, which was why they were hanging out in the hotel room, still alive. Still breathing.

Still not sure what to say to one another. The tension was too much for Peyton. She couldn't take it anymore, hating the way they tiptoed around each other trying not to rock the boat.

"Just yell at me and get it over with."

Stretched out on one of the two beds, Ellis looked up from his new phone. He was sending Josh or Chase a text, firming up plans for tomorrow. His brows had also shot up in surprise. Apparently he'd thought that they would do this forever.

"Why might I want to yell at you?"

He wanted to play it that way? Like it had never happened?

"Because of what happened last night."

Setting his cell down on the bed, he turned to give her his attention. "Let me ask you a question. If I was angry with you, what would that accomplish? Would that change your mind? I doubt it."

It wouldn't but it would make her feel less guilty.

She wasn't even sure how to begin. "I wasn't kind last night."

His lips twisted in a sort of smile. "The world isn't kind, princess, so don't sweat it. You only told the truth. I can't fault you for that."

"You should expect better from your friends. You should definitely expect better from me."

"I'm not mad at you."

She believed him. Ellis rarely lost his temper. For real. He'd growl and complain but he was always in control.

"But you're not happy with me."

His head fell back onto the headboard so he was staring at

the ceiling. "You're not going to let this go, are you? Can we just forget about it? I'm not much for picking at a scab until I bleed."

"It's just…"

She cared about him.

"It's just I don't want things to be like this," she said lamely. "This is awful."

He'd risen from the bed and walked over to the window, lifting the edge of the curtains an inch or two to look outside. "Actually I've had some time to think about this and I think you're right. We wouldn't work. We come from two different worlds, princess, and no one knows that more than I do. I've been fooling myself but you brought me back to reality. It's better if we're just protector and protectee."

She'd managed to do all that. Amazing. She rarely convinced anyone of anything but somehow he'd come to the conclusion she was a snob.

"That's not what I said," she protested. "I simply said you made me feel weak."

He dropped the curtain and turned to face her, his blue eyes an icy gray. "I don't think that's any better. In fact, it sounds a hundred times worse."

Crisscrossing her legs under her, she sat up on the mattress. He wasn't going to make this easy for her and frankly, why should he? She was the one that screwed up. She was going to have to take a few chances to make this right. He might respond or he might tell her to jump in a cold lake but she had to try.

"Will you sit down and hear me out?" she asked, watching his expression closely for any rejection. "There are things I need to tell you."

For a moment it looked like he was going to refuse but with a soft sigh, he came to sit down on the bed opposite hers. "I'm listening."

Sort of impatiently. but this was the best she could hope for under the circumstances.

"First of all, we do not come from two different worlds. I lead a very normal existence. I do laundry, I go to the grocery store, I fix dinner. I'm just like everyone else."

He snorted. "Except with millions of dollars. Let's face it, princess, you don't have to do any of those things if you don't want to. That's what separates us. You have choices most people can only dream about."

"I can't argue that," she said honestly. "But you keep calling me princess and I need you to know that I am far and away not even close to that. I don't spend my days at the spa and wear jewels and gowns. I'd rather hang out at home, order a pizza, and watch a movie."

"That's not why I call you princess." Ellis shook his head. "I call you that because sometimes you seem like you live in another place and time, as if the real world hasn't touched even though it's been fucking cruel. I don't know how you manage to keep your innocence when the universe seems bound and determined to strip it away and replace it with cynicism."

That made her smile. "The ability to compartmentalize my life. It comes in handy at times like this. If you had my upbringing, you'd be good at it too. This is a good segue, actually. About that whole weak thing…let me explain."

His entire expression closed down and she wished she could ignore this conversation but it had to be done. She had to help him understand.

"It's my mother," she choked out, her throat tightening. Talking about her family had never been easy.

"Your mother?" he echoed. "She's nothing like you."

"I'm not so sure," Peyton smiled sadly. "I think at one point in her life she might have been happy too but those days are gone. She's a shell of a human being, Ellis. Being with my father has drained whatever joy and energy out of her that she had."

Ellis scratched his chin. "Your father is...kind of intense."

"I don't want to end up like my mother. I don't want to end up weak, a mere shadow of the man in my life."

"That sounds like a good plan." He frowned and shook his head. "I'm not sure what this has to do with us though."

"I feel weak with you, and I'm scared to end up like my mother."

Chapter Thirteen

ELLIS HAD TO pick his chin up off of the floor. Peyton truly believed that being with him would make her like her mother. She did live in a world all of her own. The reality was far different.

"But I don't care about that anymore," she declared, her deep blue eyes filled with emotion. "After what happened to us today, the thought of being apart from you is unbearable. You're the single most important person in my life, Ellis. I cannot lose you. I think…I might be falling in love with you."

He'd dreamed of hearing those exact words from her pretty pink lips but not like this. That universe that had been messing with the women was branching out and taking him on now.

"Thank you…I think?"

Rearing back, she couldn't hide the hurt on her face. The pain he hadn't meant to inflict but… Hell, what was he supposed to say?

He reached across the divide and picked up her hand in his. "Listen to me, princess, what you said…damn, I barely know what to say. You have to know how I feel about you…how I've felt practically since the first moment I laid eyes on you. It's been inside of me fighting its way out and I've tried to keep it to myself knowing that you weren't ready—"

"But I am," she protested, her fingers tightening painfully on his. "I feel the same."

If only he could believe that.

"Let me review what you just said to me. You're falling in love with me and you don't care if you become a mindless robot like your mother. You're okay with that. You also said that you realized it when we were in danger, which makes me wonder if this love is more gratitude and fear of being alone. No matter what I won't abandon you, not when you need me."

Pink suffused her fair skin and she tugged her hand away to press those same fingers against her hot cheeks. "I didn't mean for it to come out like that."

He couldn't hold back the smile at her confession. "I think perhaps both of us have an issue or two when it comes to saying what we truly mean. Let's start at the beginning. Why do you think being with me will turn you into your mother?"

Her gaze dropped to the comforter. "You have such a big personality, Ellis. Let's face it, I fade into the background when we're together. If that happens now think about how it will be twenty or thirty years from now."

He'd laugh out loud if she wasn't so damn serious. "You're no wallflower, and there's no fading. You're a strong woman, Peyton, and when you walk into a room people notice. I said you were fierce and I meant it. Shit, I noticed the first moment I met you. Why in God's name do you think you're like your mother?"

Her silence spoke volumes and he had an idea who had put that image in her brain.

"Jesus H. Christ, was it your family? Did they say you were like her? I should have punched your father in the face when I had the chance."

Her fingers plucked at the hem of a pillowcase. "It was my tenth birthday. Father said I looked just like my mother."

"And?"

"That we were like twins. He called us *two peas in a pod.* Even then I knew I didn't want to be like her, or them."

Scraping his hands down his face, he realized he was going to have to try to undo damage that had been festering for over twenty years.

"Babe, parents say shit like that but they don't necessarily mean it. Sure, you and your mother are both blonde and blue-eyed with a strong family resemblance, but that's where it ends. He probably said it because little girls often want to grow up to be their mothers from what I understand. He wanted you to picture yourself as her but honey, you are not like her. You already said it yourself. You're no princess. Wasn't it you that bummed around Europe pissing off your parents before you got married?"

Finally a smile. "Yes, they hated that."

"And wasn't it you that wore old blue jeans and t-shirts when they wanted you to buy designer clothes?"

"I did that. It made my mother crazy. She'd ask why I dressed like a hobo as if she'd ever seen one in real life."

"So you're nothing like your mother," he said. "She might be quiet and retiring but you were ready to kick some ass this morning. You would have done it too."

"I'd kick your ass if it needed it," she said quietly, still not looking directly at him.

"I know you would and I would probably deserve it. You are your own woman, Peyton. You are not your mother. And I am not your father. Not by a long shot." This was about something other than being scared that she was a limp noodle. "Maybe you're scared of something else. Maybe it's not about this."

She did look up then, her eyes glittering with tears. "Say what you mean. You don't normally have this much trouble speaking your mind."

"I was only thinking of your feelings." He took a deep breath. "You're scared, so you're grabbing onto every reason on the planet. Greg was an asshole and treated you like shit. Your mother is a weakling who lives in the shadow of your overbearing father. Pick a third reason and fill in the blank. Maybe you're just scared because being in love and in a relationship is a fucking frightening thing to do. Commitment is hard and it didn't go so well last time. If you think about it, it's kind of smart to be wary. Did you worry about being weak when you married Greg?"

She tilted her head, considering his question. "I was so young I'm not sure I worried about much of anything back then. I thought he and I would live this bohemian artist lifestyle, traveling all over Europe. I was excited about the future, getting away from my parents." Her shoulders slumped. "I married for the wrong reasons. I married the wrong man."

He slid off of the bed and knelt on the floor in front of her. "I'm not asking you to marry me if that's what you're worried about. I'm not sure I'm the marrying kind. But if that artist lifestyle stuff is something you still want then I am not the man for you. I'm a cop and I go in to work every day. I work long hours and I sometimes forget to pay attention to other things. And people. It's not just what I do—it's who I am."

"I don't care about that–"

He waved away her protests. She needed to truly think about what they'd said tonight.

"I do. I care a hell of a lot because I don't want you to regret us down the road. I believe that you have feelings for me, and I know that I do for you. I think you need to really think about what you want. The kind of life you want to lead, the kind of man that will make you happy. Stop worrying about your mother or Greg and simply take control and decide what you want to be. I might fit in, but I might not. You have the power here, Peyton. Not me, your father, your mother, or Greg."

He weaved their fingers together and lifted her hands to press chaste kisses on the knuckles. He wouldn't go any further. It had to be her decision.

"I think that's the nicest refusal any woman has heard from a man."

Chuckling, he shook his head. "Because I wasn't turning you down. I'm simply delaying it a little. I'll still be here if you decide you want me. It just has to be for the right reasons."

Not because she was scared or grateful. Not because she didn't want to run her own life.

Being chivalrous sucked. He wanted to take her into his arms and keep her there but he couldn't do that. It had to be right...for both of them.

PEYTON JUST WANTED to crawl into bed and sleep for a hundred years. She hadn't rested well at the hotel in Oxford, too keyed up after what they'd been through. They'd decided to leave after only one night, Ellis practically pawing the ground to get back to the States and his familiar stomping grounds. His tension and stress level had been off the charts the entire time they'd been in the UK but now that their plane had touched down in Clearwater, his shoulders weren't as rigid and his jaw wasn't as clenched. He was still moody as hell but at least he wasn't going to have a stroke because of that.

The private airstrip was dark with only a few people bustling by them, taking care of the plane. Willow had arranged for her housekeeper to drop off one of her vehicles so they wouldn't have to take a taxi late at night. Just as she'd promised there was a small SUV waiting for them, keys under the passenger side floor mat. Ellis palmed the keys and motioned for Peyton to climb in. "Let's get out of here. I'll feel better when we're at the safe house."

It had been decided that the best place for them to hide out was the home Peyton's mother had told them about. If it was truly a secret, it seemed like the best place to lie low.

"Maybe I should drive?" Smiling, she held out her hand. "Since I know my way around this area and you...don't."

He tossed her the keys with a growl. "I guess that's okay, although you could easily direct me."

"What is it about the male animal and being driven? Does it

mess with your testosterone level?"

"It's like having your mommy drive you to school."

He'd been in a rotten mood since escaping London. Tense, grouchy, easy to bait. This time, though, she didn't think it was all her and her wayward emotions. This bad attitude was courtesy of her friendly neighborhood new world order secret society. Ellis was pissed off that they'd been run out of the city and he wasn't taking it well. In the last thirty-six hours she'd tried to make it her mission to take his mind off of things as much as possible. It hadn't been easy, stuck in one room for hours on end except when they left to get something to eat. She'd taken to telling him stories about her adventures when she was traveling about Europe and all the interesting people she'd met.

Gratefully sliding into the driver's seat, she tossed her purse and small carry-on over her shoulder and into the back seat. "I'll get us there in one piece. Do you think they know we've left?"

Always that nebulous *they*. Peyton wasn't even sure she knew who *they* were. Was it the good faction of Evandria or the rogue? Was it both? Was there even a good faction or were both sides obsessed with power? Her head hurt just thinking about it.

"I'm not sure. I never felt like we were being followed in Oxford or when we went to the airport to leave. Maybe they think we're lying low in London or somewhere near there and will turn up eventually. I don't think our presence here in the US will be much of a secret for long, though. The pilot filed a flight plan, so it's not like we could sneak back into the country."

Sighing, she pulled two ibuprofen from her pocket and popped them into her mouth, chasing them with some water from her bottle before starting the car and pulling away from the airport. The traffic was light this time of night.

"Are you going to let them know we touched down?" she asked.

"Done. I sent Chase a text as soon as we landed. I thought I'd get an answer by the time we made it through customs but maybe they're asleep."

That didn't sound right. Chase and Josh had been jumpy about Peyton and Ellis traveling back on their own. She would have thought they'd be pacing the floor until wheels on the plane touched the tarmac.

"It only took five minutes to get through customs. There wasn't a line. Why don't you text them again?"

For once Ellis didn't argue with her, instead tapping out another message. "How long will it take to get to the house?"

"About an hour and a half or so. It's off the beaten path. Remember Willow's car garage?"

Ellis nodded. "It was out in the boonies."

"This house is farther than that."

She thought she heard him mumble something along the lines of "terrific" or "awesome" but she had no doubt what he said was meant sarcastically.

"We could talk about the puzzle," she suggested when the silence became too much. Anything was better than Ellis sitting next to her worrying.

"You don't even know that it's a puzzle."

"Why would they have three addresses that all don't exist? There has to be a reason."

"Evandria's crazy. There. That's a reason."

Patience. She needed more patience to deal with Ellis when

he was like this. Ornery and stubborn, he was determined not to like anything and everyone today.

"I would think the detective in you would relish a challenge like this."

He didn't even turn from looking out of the window. "I would think by now you would realize that I don't want to fucking talk when I'm busy keeping us alive."

She'd had enough. She'd taken everything he'd dished out and then some. He wasn't even bothering with being passive-aggressive. He was aggressive without the passive.

Swerving to the shoulder of the road, she slammed on the brakes, causing him to reach out and grab the door handle while spewing out a word she wouldn't want her mother to hear.

"What the fuck are you doing?"

Putting the vehicle in park, she turned to look at him, his features barely illuminated by the lights from the dash. "I'm stopping the car. Do you know why I'm doing that?"

"Because you have a death wish?"

"Was anyone following us?"

A pause, but he still didn't turn her way. "I don't think so."

"Then stopping for a moment won't hurt anything. So let me ask again. Why do you think I pulled over?"

He was chuckling under his breath and anger surged through her veins. This wasn't funny. The relationship between the two of them had gone off the rails and he was sitting over there laughing his ass off as if it wasn't a bad thing.

"Because I'm an asshole and you're going to lecture me about proper behavior."

That was exactly what she'd been planning to do. She'd been

all geared up and ready to yell at him for being a jerk and hateful and a few other things she didn't have an adjective for. She only knew she missed the man that had been sitting by her bedside when she woke up.

He'd taken a few steps forward and she'd scrambled back.

Then she'd taken a step forward and he'd taken one back as well.

If she enjoyed dancing this might have been fun. Now they were simply two hurt people who were afraid to take a chance and put themselves out there. She put the vehicle back into gear and pressed on the accelerator. She was tired of verbally fencing with him. Exhausted. If he wanted to talk to her, he knew what to do.

"No lecture, Ellis. In fact, arguing with you is pointless. If you want to act like this, please be my guest."

They might be glad to be back in the States, but things were not harmonious. Something or someone was going to blow. And soon.

Chapter Fourteen

P EYTON'S MOTHER HAD spoken the truth. The house wasn't all that fancy. In fact, it was a little rundown, needing a coat of paint and landscaping. But it was furnished, hooked up to water and electricity, and definitely private. She'd pulled the car into the garage, although anyone driving by would be able to see the lights on. They'd be sure to keep the drapes closed.

Ellis headed straight for the kitchen with the small amount of groceries they'd been able to buy at an all-night convenience store along the way. Eventually they'd need to drive the twenty miles to the nearest grocery store but they had enough to have breakfast and lunch, plus a myriad of snack food.

She ran her finger along the surface of an end table. "I thought it would be encrusted in dust but it's not. It could use a cleaning but it's actually not that bad."

Ellis opened the refrigerator. "The fridge and freezer are clean and empty but cold too. Your mother must have a caretaker of some sort keeping up the place. Maybe they come in once or month or so."

Someone had to be caring for the home. The lawn was

mowed, although it lacked any embellishments to decorate it. The inside of the house was comfortable but it didn't look as if it had been redecorated in over forty years. An overstuffed olive green sofa with two matching chairs sat in the living room along with a coffee table and two end tables. There was a nondescript painting on one wall and a television from another century on the other. It was console style, the kind she'd seen in old photos from the sixties and seventies when televisions were furniture. Green shag carpeting finished off the retro look.

"Do you think it works?"

Ellis had finished putting away the groceries and had joined her in the living room.

She reached out and pushed the on/off button. "I seriously doubt it but there's only one way to find out."

The television made a humming sound and then suddenly flared to life.

Static and snow.

Ellis was smiling for the first time that day. Make that two days. "The television is from when they made things to last but I'm guessing it doesn't get Netflix. Maybe the rabbit ears work."

He fiddled with the antenna and the dials until a passable picture came through – an old movie on a local channel.

"I feel like we've stepped back in time," she said, her gaze taking in the room. "Like we should be eating fondue and green Jello."

Straightening, he grinned. "I swear this looks just like my childhood home right down to the harvest gold appliances in the kitchen. Man, this brings back memories."

They must be good ones from the way he was smiling. It was

funny that she'd tried to get him to lighten up but all it had taken was a seventies themed decor and an old television set.

"I'd like to hear about those memories some time."

His head jerked toward her as if surprised she was even standing there. He'd been lost in the past. "I doubt you'd find them all that interesting. I had a fairly boring childhood."

She shook her head. "Not from the way you're smiling. There must have been something."

"Just silliness." He shrugged but the smile was still there. "Kids doing stupid shit. Riding bikes all over the neighborhood and getting dirty. Eating bologna and mustard sandwiches on soft white bread. Watching 'The A-Team' with my family. Stuff like that."

Now she was smiling too and it felt wonderful not to have that wall of tension between them. "'The A-Team'? What else did you watch?"

"'Magnum PI' was my favorite but I watched other things. Why? What did you watch when you were a kid?"

She was younger than Ellis. "'The X-Files'. 'Twin Peaks'."

"You liked those intellectual shows. It figures."

"Intellectual? They were just interesting."

He tapped the top of the television. "Compared to 'The A-Team', those shows were intellectual. I liked action, you liked to think."

"Ellis, I think you just summed up our entire relationship."

His gaze dropped to the ugly shag carpeting and he scraped his fingers through his short, dark hair. "Listen, I'm sorry I've been such an asshole. I'm just worried and stressed but I shouldn't take it out on you."

She looked around the empty house. "There's no else to take it out on so I guess I'm the lucky person. Seriously, I was mad earlier but I'm not now. I know that you have a lot weighing on your shoulders and it's going to take its toll. We just need to be nicer to each other even when we don't feel like it."

"You're right. Lately it just feels like nothing is easy. Every fucking thing is a struggle. Even the day to day activities like going to the store or getting on a plane have become a huge production."

Because of her and her issues. She didn't want him to go but she cared enough for him to want him to be happy. And safe. With her, he didn't appear to be either of those things.

"You don't have to do this anymore." She wanted to reach out to him but she didn't dare. "You've gone above and beyond and no one would blame you if you decided to forget all about this and just go back to your regular life. I wouldn't think any less of you if you did. You've earned some time off."

Chuckling, Ellis shook his head. "This I want to do. I want to bring down Evandria so badly I can taste it. I dream about it, I'm not going anywhere. We finish this together—even if at the end you and I are finished too."

"We haven't even begun."

His expression was gentle, more like the man she'd known when she was in the hospital.

"Yes, we have, whether you want to admit it or not. I've said it before and I'll say it again. The future is happening now while you're not paying attention. This house might be one giant step back into the past, but you can't live there forever."

Turning, he walked back into the kitchen, leaving her standing there.

Alone. Is that how she wanted to live her life?

PEYTON DUMPED HALF of the scrambled eggs on each plate before retrieving the toast from the toaster. For once she'd woken up first and had decided to fix breakfast while Ellis showered. In the bright light of day, the kitchen looked cheerier than it had last night. Maybe it was the addition of food or the heavenly smell of freshly brewed coffee. Or perhaps it was that she and Ellis had come to some sort of truce last night. She hated it when they were at odds with one another.

That in and of itself should have been a huge clue. As she'd fallen asleep last night, she'd replayed his words over and over in her head.

They'd already begun, but here she was stubbornly standing still as the world sped on by. She didn't want anyone else besides Ellis and she didn't want him to want anyone else either. He was right. They were already in a relationship, although undefined. It might be time to put a label on the darn thing.

"Something smells good."

Him. After his shower he always smelled wonderful, but she had a feeling he was talking about the food. His dark hair was still wet and he'd pulled on a pair of khaki cargo shorts and a navy blue t-shirt that showed off his wide shoulders and flat stomach.

"The coffee is ready and so is breakfast. I hope you're hungry. I set a mug next to the coffeemaker for you."

He filled it and slid into a chair at the Formica table. "Thanks, I'm always hungry—you know that. Did you sleep well?"

It had been late – or early in the morning – when they'd finally turned in for the night; Peyton in the master bedroom and Ellis right next door.

"I did, but you probably knew that. How many times did you get up and check on me?"

"Only twice. I was pretty tired myself, although I caught some z's on the plane. For a house that hasn't been lived in for a long time, that mattress was pretty comfortable. I'm kind of getting the feeling that your mother uses this place on occasion."

They'd forgotten to buy butter last night. Peyton mentally added it to her growing shopping list.

"I can't imagine when she would have. She and Dad already have a house in Midnight Blue Beach and others in every major city in the world. Why would she stay here?"

He chuckled and took a healthy bite of his eggs. "I'm getting the feeling you think this place is a dump."

Actually it was kind of cute and cozy. With updated furnishings it wouldn't be a bad place to live.

"I don't think that but my mother might. She thinks the world is filled with mansions, chateaus, villas, and five-star hotels. A ranch house in the middle of nowhere isn't a place she'd visit for rest and relaxation. In fact, I'm not sure what her family used this house for. She grew up on an estate in Rhode Island."

"An investment? If they bought this place in 1970 or thereabouts they probably paid less than twenty-thousand for it, maybe much less. With the surrounding land it's worth more now."

"Maybe," she conceded. "It was weird when she said that my father didn't know about this place. I wonder why she kept it a secret?"

Ellis cleaned the last bite of eggs from his plate. "I would imagine living with your father isn't easy. Maybe she comes here to hide out and just be by herself for a few days?"

Peyton's mother did travel extensively and sometimes without her husband. It was possible.

But not probable.

"That's a theory but I'm still not seeing her staying here."

"There may be things about your mother that you don't know."

Peyton had learned more than her share of secrets in the past month or so.

"Somehow I don't think that my mother pretending to be a 1970s housewife is one of them, but I've been wrong before. In fact, all this summer has taught me is that I don't know anything about the people in my life."

Ellis pushed his plate away and took a sip of his coffee. "I have a theory about that. Maybe it's not as important to know the people in our lives as it is to know ourselves. Kind of deep for this early in the morning."

Now he was just being a shit. "That's groovy, man. Peace."

Laughing, he reached for her plate. "You look all wealthy and uptight and then you act like a comedienne. I said something moving and profound and you shit all over it. Are you going to finish those eggs?"

She pushed the plate closer to him. "I am not but the toast is all mine. I can make more if you're still hungry. As for being funny, you're the only person in the world that I could make that remark to. Everybody else wouldn't get it or would be insulted. But you...you laugh."

He ate the last two bites of her eggs in quick succession. "What does that tell you about me?"

Her heart lurched against her ribs and she took a deep breath of courage. "That you're my best friend and that you're special."

He grinned and waggled his eyebrows. "You bet your sweet ass I am."

"I've missed you," she said softly. "Welcome back."

"Was I missing? Should we put my picture on a milk carton?"

He knew exactly what she was talking about.

"You were, but you're here now and that's all that matters."

There was a moment as she gazed into his blue eyes that the world was safe, warm, and all was right. Unfortunately, it didn't last long. His phone buzzed in the background and he had to answer it, breaking that little bit of happiness they'd found this morning.

"Hey Chase, what's going on?"

It wasn't good. With each passing minute, Ellis's expression grew darker and more dangerous until she thought he was going to jump out of that chair and grab the first plane back to his friends. She grabbed onto his arm to try to calm him but the laughter he'd so easily displayed was long gone, leaving an angry and agitated man in its place.

"Get the hell out of there," he said, his teeth gritted together. "I'm guessing no place is safe."

Ellis hopped to his feet and began to pace the small kitchen. "I get what you're saying. The dogs scared them off and they're a great burglar alarm, but clearly they know where you are and they're either trying to scare you or trying to grab the women. Neither is a great option, to be truthful. I know you think you're safest there but now that they know the dogs are guarding you they'll just figure something else out. They'll ambush you outside the grocery store or even in the driveway. I can't tell you what to do but I think a change in venue is in order. Hell, take the dogs with you. You can always come here. I don't think anyone knows where we are."

Clearly, it wasn't safe at Chase and Josh's anymore. Peyton refilled their coffee as it looked like they'd need the caffeine to deal with whatever had gone down in Williamsburg. If Ellis was inviting them down here, it had to be bad.

There was a little more discussion before Ellis hung up, muttering under his breath. He tossed the phone on the table and dragged his fingers through his hair again.

"They had some visitors about four in the morning. The dogs ran them off but Chase and Josh could see footprints around both houses. Lots of rain in the last twenty-four hours made the earth soft enough they were able to make four distinct sets of footprints but there may have been more. Considering Evandria was trying to get you, it's not surprising they were going for Bailey and Willow but I am shocked that they had the brass balls to stroll right up to the house."

Peyton had been feeling almost comfortable in the safe house, but that had been shot to hell. Ellis was right. Nowhere was safe. They'd shaken up Evandria and now the organization –

or some part of it – was hitting back.

"Are they okay?"

"Shaken up but fine. Now they're trying to decide whether to leave or stay. There are good arguments on both sides but the desperation of Evandria is beginning to make me think they're not playing it as cool as they have in the past. This trying to grab you off the streets of London is amateur hour. And now this? These actions aren't worthy of a world class secret society. This is thug level behavior."

"So Archer Caldwell was the brains behind Evandria? I find that hard to believe."

"Hardly," Ellis scoffed. "What I'm saying is that I don't think Evandria itself is behind this. I think there might be a few individuals who feel threatened and they've gone out on their own. Whether they're part of the rogue faction I don't know, but it doesn't feel like the smart, slick Evandria we've all come to know and love."

She handed him his coffee cup. "So what now?"

"We go to the store and stock up on food so we can hole up here for days if we need to. In fact, we should get extra in case the others have to move in with us. Then we sit tight and let things die down a little bit. Let them think we've given up." He smiled but it was more evil than happy. "But we never give up. It's when they're this nervous that we know we're doing something right."

Chapter Fifteen

"IT WAS COLONEL Mustard in the library with the pistol," Ellis announced, a smug smile on his face. They were sitting on the floor of the living room, a board game between them on the coffee table, while the television played softly in the background.

Pursing her lips, she handed him the little folder. "So check to see if you're right. But just because you're a detective in real life doesn't mean you're one in a game. The skills are not transferable."

After coming home from the grocery store where they'd loaded up as if expecting a blizzard, they'd quickly become bored. There was no Wi-Fi at the house so they had to use their phones to read email or look anything up. Peyton had gone digging through the tall cabinet in the living room and found board games that looked as old as the house. She hadn't been able to convince Ellis to play Mystery Date but he'd been all over Clue the minute he saw it.

Hiding the cards behind his large hand, a smile bloomed on his face. "I'm right. I won."

Sighing, she slapped her pencil down on the table. "You're a sore winner."

"How can I be a sore winner when all I said was *I won*? Maybe you're a sore loser."

She began to pack up the game. "I am not a sore loser."

"Are you quite sure? Because I feel sorry for those game pieces, the way you're manhandling them. Admit it, princess, you have a competitive streak a mile wide. Personally I think it's great. Why play a game unless you want to win?"

He would think like that. Ellis Hunter wanted to win, be better than everyone else. It was in his DNA and he was proud of it.

"Winning is not important."

He cleared his throat, obviously trying not to laugh at her. "It's all about how you play the game."

She smacked the lid on the box and pushed it out of her way. "It is."

"No, it's not. That's just something they tell little kids so they won't throw building blocks at each other. But we're adults and we know that winning matters."

She walked over to the cabinet and slid the box back in, perusing the other games. Maybe Yahtzee or Monopoly?

"Ladies don't care about things like that."

His mouth had dropped open. "Is that your mother talking? I can hear her saying something like that along with not to get your dress dirty and to always be polite to grownups. Am I right?"

Too right for comfort.

She snagged the Monopoly box and placed it on the table

between them. "Sometimes I'll be talking and my mother will start coming out of my mouth. It's disturbing."

"Sometimes I'll say something that my dad always used to say. I think that's normal."

Sitting cross-legged on a cushion, Peyton opened up the game. "Have you rejected your parents and everything they stand for?"

"Not lately but I've been meaning to get around to it. I've just been so busy and with the holidays coming up and all…"

She unfolded the board and then grabbed the top hat piece. She was always the top hat.

"Very funny. I'm serious here. I've turned my back on my parents' life but every now and then a part of the past won't leave me alone. My mother especially. She had so many rules about how a well-brought up lady should conduct herself. Jensen didn't have near as many things to remember. I wanted to be a boy for the longest time."

His gaze raked her up and down, making her blood pound heavily in her veins. "You're no boy, that's for sure. As for your mother, she probably just wanted to make sure you graduated high school and didn't become a heroin junkie, knocking over liquor stores for money."

"I doubt my mother even knows what heroin is. Her dream for me was to find a nice rich man and settle down. All I wanted to do was the opposite."

She started doling out the money but he held up a hand. "Wait a minute. Why do you get to be the bank?"

"I'm always the bank."

"So am I."

She slid the plastic money tray off to the side and then stacked the property deeds next to it. "How about a compromise? We'll have a modern bank that's self-service."

A grin spread across his face. He'd smiled more since they arrived here than he had the entire time in London. "Do you trust me?"

That was an easy question.

"With my life and even with cash." She wagged her finger at him. "But I'll be watching."

"I wouldn't expect anything less."

Monopoly wasn't a quick sort of game and it took the better part of four hours before it was over. They'd taken a few breaks here and there but it was finally done.

"Hand it over," she said with glee. "I have a hotel on Park Place and it's going to cost you."

He placed his two remaining railroads on top of his remaining cash. "That's all I have. You've cleaned me out. You're a real barracuda when it comes to business, princess. Did you learn that from daddy?"

"I might have picked up a few tips. I guess I win. What's next?"

Ellis stretched easily, finally standing and yawning. "I get to pick the next game."

"We need to eat dinner first. Do you think we can take a walk too?"

He wanted to say yes, she could see it in his eyes but in the end he shook his head. "I don't think so. Not with the intruders at Josh and Chase's homes. We went to the store because we had to but if it's not necessary I think we need to stay inside. I'm so sorry, honey."

He was and he was right too. They shouldn't be outside. She was getting a little cabin fever staying inside though so it was a good thing they'd also picked up some wine while they were shopping.

"I know and it's okay. I was just hoping. I'll go make dinner. It'll give me something to do."

Ellis talked to Chase and Josh again while she cooked a simple dinner of spaghetti and garlic bread. That was one of the great things about Ellis. He wasn't picky about his food.

He insisted on doing the dishes so she settled onto the couch with her glass of red wine and the local news on the television. The picture wasn't any good but the sound was fine and the overly happy weatherman said it was going to rain the next day.

The drone of the newscasters and the alcohol made her pleasantly relaxed. The day with Ellis had been good. Like before but even better now that she was feeling more herself. The more time she spent with him, the more she liked him which was a surprise. In the past she'd found that familiarity bred…well, not contempt, but it didn't nurture and grow deep feelings for a man. Of course, this man had thrown all of that on its head. So engrossed in her thoughts, she didn't hear Ellis until he was right beside her, taking the glass from her hand and setting it on the end table.

"Are you ready for bed?"

Yes. Maybe. Wait, what was the question?

"Bed?"

An image of Ellis and herself in a king-sized bed flashed through her mind.

"You look tired," he explained. "Did you want to go to bed early?"

She shook her head. "No, if I go to bed now I'll be up at three in the morning. I was just enjoying the quiet. Time to think and all."

"What were you thinking about?"

It was a perfectly natural question that she absolutely didn't want to answer but she found herself doing it anyway.

"You."

His brows flew up and eyes widened. "Me? What about me?"

Peyton waved the question away. "Just stuff."

"Stuff," he dutifully repeated, his lips twitching with mirth. "What kind of stuff? Specifically."

"For one thing, how nosy you are."

"Fine, don't tell me. I'll just make it all up in my mind."

That sounded worse but she'd have to take her chances.

"Are you going to pick out a game?" she asked, wanting to steer the conversation away to another topic. "There's about a dozen in that stack. I think the Game of Life is in there."

"I'll pass," he groaned, padding over to the cabinet. "Aren't we kind of doing that every day?"

She could hear him pulling out all of the boxes one by one. "Did you find anything you wanted to play?"

"Got it." He came to stand in front of her, holding up a game. "Let's do this."

One look and she almost hopped up from the couch and hid behind it. There was no way. She couldn't do this. Not with him.

Not Twister.

THERE WAS A special place in hell for whomever had designed Twister. What had been good, wholesome fun for a child was much more suggestive and even erotic for an adult.

After Peyton had admitted she'd never played the game, Ellis had flipped over the box lid and read her the rules. There weren't many. Basically the first person who couldn't make the move on the spinner was the loser. She'd seen enough of the game on television to know that he had a tremendous advantage with his long arms and legs. That he was going to win was a foregone conclusion.

That she was going to be a complete and utter mess by the time they were done was also an absolute. The fact that she was aroused by Ellis had never been in question, only what she was going to do about it. If anything. It was beginning to feel like they were inevitable, careening toward a collision that would change her – and him – forever. But first she had to survive this game.

The first few moves hadn't been difficult. Right hand red. Left foot green, and so on. It was when they were about a dozen or more spins in and they were beginning to get tangled up pretty good that things started to heat up. Every time Ellis switched position, he seemed to find a reason to touch her even if it was only a brief second, and every time he did she had to concentrate not to fall into a puddle of want on the floor. In the past he'd been careful to keep his distance but lately he'd begun to move closer, initiating contact more often even if it was an act as simple as helping her on with her raincoat or giving her a hand in and out of the taxi.

Reaching for the spinner, he spun for her since she couldn't reach. She had her left foot on green and her right foot on red, her right hand on blue and her left hand on yellow. So far, so good but the new spin had her right hand on red. Normally that would have been totally fine except that he was already on the two closest red circles which meant she was going to have to stretch out even more to get her hand there.

Over or under? It would probably be easier to go under Ellis who was on all fours facing her left. If she tried to go over him she was fairly sure her legs and arms wouldn't be long enough.

"I'm just going to…" She began to slide underneath his torso and he tried to arch his back to ease her way but the extra inches didn't help much. This wasn't going to be easy. Already her body was tuned to his every breath or twitch. She could feel the heat radiate from his skin and smell his masculine scent, spicy and warm. Taking a deep lungful of him, her fingers itched to abandon the game and explore him instead, running over every dip and plane of his arms and shoulders.

"Take your time," he cautioned. "You've got this."

Inching her hand across the plastic, she held her breath until she was touching the red circle. But now that she was breathing again, she noticed that she was pressed up against Ellis's front.

The front of his pants.

And he was obviously enjoying the game. He had chosen it after all, so he had to have known this was going to happen. Sneaky. She ought to be mad at him but she'd agreed to play.

Face it, I hoped this would happen.

It was just like him to help her out like this. He'd known what a quandary she was in, going back and forth, and always chickening out. He'd made it easy. Play the game or feign exhaustion? He'd given her every opportunity to say no but her tacit agreement was a green light for more. More touching. More light flirting. More of them. Less drama and angst.

Thank you, Ellis.

He spun for his turn and was able to lift off of her, placing himself to the right, but as he moved he brushed against her, sending tingles through her veins like bubbles in champagne. A few more moves and they found themselves facing each other, his lips mere inches away.

Her tight throat made it difficult to speak. "Can you, um, spin for me?"

The words came out kind of squeaky but he didn't remark on it. Reaching behind him, he quickly spun the wheel and the arrow landed on left foot blue.

She could do this. All she had to do was slide her foot to the left. Easy-peasy.

His mouth was turned up into a half-smile as she slowly made her move, her gaze following her toes all the way to her destination. When she looked up in triumph, he'd somehow leaned closer and his lips brushed hers, ghosting over them so lightly at first she'd thought she imagined it. It was when he did it again that she realized she wasn't dreaming. This was real and they were kissing. At last. All the doubts that had been swirling around in her head and driving her crazy had dissolved the moment his lips touched hers. The future was happening now and she didn't want to miss a minute of it.

His mouth was firm but gentle, not demanding a response but cajoling one. He tasted like the red wine they'd enjoyed earlier and she swore she could get drunk simply kissing him. His tongue slid along her lower lip and she opened to him as they tumbled to the floor in a tangle of arms and legs. They broke apart, giggling like kids, and she reached up to cup his face in her hands.

"Thank you."

Nuzzling her with his nose, he pressed a light kiss to her cheekbone, then each eyelid, making it very hard to catch her breath.

"You're welcome, princess."

She ran her hands down his neck and over his shoulders, finally feeling his muscles under her palms. "Do you even know why I thanked you?"

He'd been patient. Not perfect, of course, but he'd put up with so much of her back and forth. The mixed signals and the indecision.

He smiled and her stomach fluttered in response. Maybe this was why he didn't smile often. If he did, women would be falling at his feet wherever he went.

"I do know and it wasn't easy. You're worth it."

She nudged his leg with her foot. "You think you know everything about me."

He bent his head and ran his tongue up the cord of her neck until she was digging her fingers into his biceps. "I don't, but I do think finding out is going to be fun."

"What if you find out things you don't like?"

He lifted up slightly. "We already have. We've practically

been in each other's pockets for weeks and we've managed not to commit murder. It hasn't been a day at the beach but it has been fun. You have to admit that, princess."

Pulling him closer, she pressed her lips to his until they were both breathless, hearts pounding. "You're the most fun I've ever had."

He shook his head as if denying her statement. "I've never been accused of being fun."

"You are now. Will you kiss me again?"

Chapter Sixteen

E LLIS MISSED READING the news while drinking his morning coffee. He didn't dare leave the house just to get a paper so he was stuck either watching the local news on the old television or scrolling through it on the cell phone. He couldn't help but wonder if there were any articles regarding Archer Caldwell, good or bad. Now that he was in Evandria custody, how was he running his personal businesses? Had anyone noticed that he wasn't around?

"You don't like French toast?"

Peyton's question dragged his attention away from the phone and back to her. She looked especially beautiful this morning, dressed in light blue shorts and a white eyelet t-shirt, her pale blonde hair pulled back into a ponytail. In fact, she was the most beautiful woman he'd ever seen in his life. A woman he'd made out with like a teenager last night.

"I love it, I'm just distracted waiting for the others. They should have been here thirty minutes ago."

Late last night the decision had been made to leave Williamsburg and come down here to the safe house. Ellis was as sure as he could be that they weren't being watched so it only made sense. Six of them plus six dogs was going to make this place feel awfully small but being safe was the highest priority.

"They said they were going to stop for more groceries," Peyton reminded him. "That's probably what slowed them down. They'll be here."

"It's my job to worry."

She smiled and picked up his fork, holding it in front of him. "It's my job to keep you calm. Eating your breakfast would be a good start. I slaved over a hot stove for that."

He accepted the fork and their fingers brushed, sending bolts of electricity straight up his arm. He doubted she had any idea the effect she had on him.

"Did I mention how pretty you look this morning?"

The mouthful of French toast paused halfway to her lips. "Ellis Hunter, are you trying to flirt with me? Because if you are, it's working. Thank you."

He shifted in his chair. "I admit that flirting and wooing are not my strong suit but I can try."

Her blue eyes were warm and bright. "I think you're doing just fine."

They ate in silence until their plates were clean. Ellis pushed his away and dabbed at his mouth with the napkin. "You know they're going to notice. This. Us. Are you prepared for that?"

Ellis didn't want to keep it a secret but he wasn't a yell it from the roof kind of guy either. Chase and Josh, however, would take one look at him and know what was up. Ellis didn't look at anyone else the way he looked at Peyton. No one had managed to get to him the way she had and he wasn't fooling his friends trying to act cool.

Sighing, she nodded. "I think so. I just hope Willow and Bailey understand that we're doing this at our own pace. I want them to respect that."

They hadn't slept together last night. They might not tonight either. That was fine with Ellis. As she'd said, they'd proceed at their own pace.

"I'm sure if you explain that they will. I'm guessing that Chase and Josh have told them that I don't have the best track record with women. They probably don't think I'm much of a bargain."

Picking up their empty plates, she carried them over to the sink. "You haven't had many serious relationships?"

"That would be an understatement. My career has been everything to me and women rarely have the patience for the strange hours that a detective works. If someone dies in the middle of the night, I get out of bed and go to the crime scene. I don't get to wait for the morning commute."

Picking up the coffee pot, she refilled her mug and then his. "When you go out in the middle of the night do you drink, gamble, or generally chase women? Marry them and have a secret family?"

"No, I do not, but you need to have higher standards than that for a man, princess. Make the guy toe the line."

"That guy would be you," she smirked. "I draw the lines around here so I'll let you know when you have a toe over it. In the meantime, I'm not too worried about a workaholic. It would be a nice change. I think the big thing for me is once this is all over, I need to find something that fills my days. Something I'm passionate about so I'm not sitting around waiting for you to get off of work."

"It sounds good in theory. What kind of things are you passionate about? I know you like art."

She nodded, settling back down into the kitchen chair. "I am, but I think my real love has always been photography. I used to take photos all of the time and wanted to have my own gallery showing someday."

"I don't know what's involved with that but it sounds like an ambitious goal."

A smile curved her full lips. "I'd love to take some pictures of you at work. All the cops, actually. Real life police work with real life police. Do you think I could do that?"

He rubbed the back of his neck. "It would probably be fine, but I think you don't perhaps realize how incredibly boring police work actually is."

"Do you miss it?"

She was staring down at her coffee as if it was fascinating. "Ask the real question, because I'm doing cop work right now."

She looked up, her eyes wide. "I don't want you to lose your job. What if this goes on for a long time? Eventually you're going to run out of vacation time."

Snorting, he took another sip of his coffee. "I have a hell of a lot to burn but you're right. At some point, decisions will have to be made."

"Willow suggested hiring a security firm."

He shook his head. "We quickly discarded that idea. Trust no one, remember? People can be bought and Evandria has deep pockets."

She threw up her hands. "Then what will we do? I want you to be able to do your job and I know you want to keep me safe. I'm not sure you can do both."

He'd thought about this very question, late at night after everyone was asleep. The few options they had weren't ideal but they were…possible.

"There are ways," he began slowly, not sure that this moment was the best for revealing schemes that were clearly on the insane side. "We could go underground. Get new identities and start a new life."

That she didn't laugh out loud at him was a plus. Maybe the idea wasn't as absurd as he thought it was. "New identities? I thought that was something that only happened in books and in movies."

"You'd be surprised. As a cop, I've heard of criminals getting a whole new life when they're on the run. I'm told there are specialists out there that can create a new person on the computer and insert them into databases all over the world as if they were there all along. For a price, of course."

Her brows pinched together. "You could be a cop with a fake identity?"

"Stranger things have happened. The government does stuff like this all the time for people in Witness Protection."

"I imagine they would do a better job than some criminal in a basement churning out fake passports."

Chuckling inwardly, Ellis didn't ruin Peyton's naïveté, but he was almost positive that those people were one and the same. Government guys who picked up a little cash on the side for their "retirement".

Ellis smiled. "How do you know they're in a basement?"

"I don't know—that's just how I picture it. Sweaty guys poring over ill-lit desks in a dark room, furtively hiding from the law."

Holy hell. "You've watched way too many movies."

She was quiet again and he could almost see the wheels turning in her head as she played with the handle of her coffee mug.

"You'd be giving up a lot," she finally said. "I'm not sure I could ask you to do that."

"You're not asking me," he said easily. "I thought this up on my own. Listen, let's hope it doesn't come to that, okay? But if it does, just know that I'll walk into it with you and not look back. It might be kind of cool to get a second chance at my life. Maybe I'll be smarter and more handsome next go around."

That drew a laugh out of her. "Definitely. I'd like to be taller."

He reached for her hand. "Chase, Josh, and I are going to talk about this when they get here. They're a hell of a lot smarter than I am so they will have thought about this too. I'm sure of it. My whole thinking is that we need to disappear but they could have much better plans. Let's just see how things go over the next few weeks."

The sound of a car engine outside instantly had Ellis on alert. It was probably Chase and Josh but he couldn't be too careful. "Stay here while I see who it is."

He stood but she captured his arm and pulled him down so they were face to face. Her arm went around his neck and their noses brushed just before their lips did the same. The kiss was full of hunger and he gladly let her take control of it, content to follow her lead. He was only beginning to plumb the depths of this woman's passion. Greg Nelson was a fucking idiot but his loss was Ellis's gain.

He lifted his head and enjoyed the pink on her cheeks and her slightly swollen lips. "I better go see if it's Chase and Josh before they come barging in here. I'm going to have them park their vehicle in the garage and come in the back way."

It was good his friends were here. The case had stalled, they were hiding out for their lives, and no one would tell them the truth. He needed to make something happen or they'd be stuck here going nowhere. Waiting for someone to kill them.

Chapter Seventeen

D INNER WAS EATEN and the dishes washed. The men were in the living room discussing the state of the case and Peyton was in the kitchen with Willow and Bailey, working on the puzzle. Or drinking wine and working on the puzzle. The dogs were snoozing on Josh and Willow's bed.

"Chase has been in a terrible mood these last few days," Bailey confessed, her voice low so she wouldn't be overheard by anyone but the women. "He can't get the senator to return his calls. The frustration practically radiates off of him."

Willow rolled her eyes. "As mellow as Josh is, he's even been a little testy. That whole thing where they tried to break in has him walking the house, locked and loaded. He's paranoid as hell, too. Soon he's going to be looking for the black helicopters."

Fiddling with the stem of her glass, Peyton snuck a look out of the kitchen to the living room where Ellis was deep in conversation with his friends. She wanted to know what they were talking about.

"We're all paranoid as hell," Bailey sighed. "I used to be a normal person that lived a normal life—now I can't even go to the ATM without wondering who's watching."

"Everybody," Peyton said with a grimace. "The government, the banks, and Evandria. I'm pretty sure they watch everything."

Willow looked around the old-fashioned kitchen. "Except here. There's no Wi-Fi, not even a cordless phone. There is a landline hooked to the wall but it doesn't work. There's no cable television, only rabbit ears. This safe house is seriously old school. Good job on finding it."

"We didn't really find it. It's my mother's, something she's apparently kept a secret from my father and everyone else."

"Did she grow up here?" Bailey asked.

The idea of that made Peyton laugh. "Not at all. She grew up on an estate in Rhode Island. Ellis and I have our theories as to why she owns this house and held on to it for so long but I think the most probable one is that it was an investment."

It was Willow's turn to frown. "If this is an investment, she needs a new property manager. No one in their right mind is going to rent this place unless they're looking to reenact the Bicentennial." She shook her head. "This has all the earmarks of a sentimental act. Maybe someone she knew and loved lived here."

"Your grandmother, maybe?" Bailey suggested. "Or a close friend?"

"My grandmother's family had big money so they wouldn't have lived here. Maybe a nanny?" Peyton mentally ran through what her mother had said about her past and realized it wasn't all that much. Just a bunch of family stuff about honor and tradition but few specifics. "As for friends, this is going to sound terrible but I don't think she has any. Not close ones. She has ladies she lunches with and sits on charity boards with, but no one that I know of that would be someone that she would confide in."

"She has to have at least one close friend," Willow declared. "Every woman does. Think back to her childhood. Did she mention anyone?"

Peyton shook her head. "I swear she didn't. I'm sure she has a close friend but she doesn't talk about it. Mother always said that ladies didn't speak of personal matters so she wouldn't mention a confidant."

Bailey's brows went up. "Maybe she had a close friend who passed away and they lived here. That would explain why you never heard about it and this house was never updated. Sort of like a shrine to their friendship."

Peyton's mother was not one for shows of sentiment but it was possible. "Maybe we could do some sort of deed search on the house and find out who owned it prior to my mother."

"That's a great idea," Willow agreed. "There has to be some sort of online search for that."

Bailey laughed and looked around the retro kitchen. "If only we had the modern convenience of the internet, but we don't even have a dishwasher."

"We do," Peyton giggled. "Ellis."

"What are you ladies laughing about in there?" Josh yelled from the living room, drawing more giggles from the three women. "We could use a chuckle."

"We were laughing about you," Willow yelled back, a smirk on her face. "You stay out there. No boys allowed in our club-house."

"Have you made any progress on the puzzle?" Bailey asked, digging cookies out of the pantry.

"None," Peyton admitted with a sigh. "As Ellis keeps reminding me, it might not even be a puzzle. It just bugs me. Why would Alex have a list of names and addresses where the streets all don't exist? It doesn't make any sense."

"None of this makes any sense," Willow replied. "As for that list, it might have made sense to Alex or he might not have even known the addresses were bogus. Toward the end he wasn't very coherent. He could have messed up those addresses because he was drunk."

"He could have," Peyton conceded. "I just think it's worth looking at."

Josh, Chase, and Ellis appeared at the entrance to the kitchen wearing grim expressions that made Peyton's stomach tighten with apprehension. Chase held up his phone and then handed it to Bailey.

"I think you need to look at your email, babe."

Although they were all using burner phones at this point, they were still checking their email occasionally. Bailey reached for her wine glass instead of the phone.

"I'm guessing you've been monitoring my inbox, so why don't you just tell me?"

"Nigel sent you an email. He wants to talk to you, to all of us," Chase replied, holding out the phone again. "Will you call him back?"

This time she did accept it. "I will. Speaker again?"

Ellis leaned against the wall. "Please. Let's try and find out where he is and what state Evandria is in. Also, see if he knows about the attempts to take you."

"And if he's aware of where we are now," Josh added. "We think we're under the radar but I'd like to know for sure."

Ellis and Chase nodded in agreement.

Nodding, Bailey dialed Nigel's number. He picked up on the third ring.

"Uncle Nigel, it's Bailey. I got your email."

"I'm glad you could call me back, child. I only have a few moments to talk though. We're very busy here getting things set up. Are your friends there?"

Ellis nodded.

"Willow and Peyton?" Bailey asked. "Yes, they're here."

"Good. I'm going to something quite unorthodox here but this situation is so out of the ordinary it seems to demand it. I'm going to invite you to Archer's trial."

Everything else Bailey was supposed to find out seemed completely unimportant. They were all huddled around the kitchen table, leaning in to catch every word Nigel Holmwood might say.

"That's…that's amazing," Bailey stuttered in surprise. "I didn't know something like that was even possible."

"It's not our usual process but clearly this is a delicate situation and we want to be sure that you see that Evandria is taking this seriously. It's tomorrow at seven sharp. Will you be here? Are you even in Florida?"

They all nodded but of course he couldn't hear them so Bailey answered out loud.

"We can be there. Is that where you are, Uncle Nigel?"

"Yes, my dear, there is much to do before tomorrow night. I

do need to go now. They'll have your information at the gate. I'll see you then."

He was gone before Bailey could ask him any more questions. Stunned, no one said anything for awhile, trying to digest what had just happened.

"It could be a huge trap," Ellis finally said. "They may not know where we are and they're trying to draw us out."

Josh crossed his arms over his chest. "Or they really are inviting us to the trial. But I doubt it's out of the goodness of their hearts. There has to be a purpose for them to do this."

"A show of Evandria power," Willow murmured. "These people are all about the power. What better way to display it than to take down their leader right in front of us and their members?"

"So what do we do?" Chase asked, frustration in his tone. "If we go, we risk being found and all that goes with that. If we stay, we miss the possibility of getting into Evandria and seeing this go down."

"Actually," Bailey piped up. "They didn't invite all of us. They invited the *three of us*."

Ellis shook his head. "Hell, no. You ladies are not going in there by yourselves."

"It's up to us," Willow said softly. "They were our husbands and this is our decision."

Peyton nodded in agreement and Ellis groaned his disapproval. She wasn't going to make his life easy and say no.

"You said so yourself that this case is at a dead-end," she pointed out. "This is our chance to make something happen. See what we can find out. I don't think we can afford to turn this down."

"You could get yourself killed," Ellis growled, his brows pulled down. "Don't ask me to stand by and let you do that."

Bailey raised her hand. "I'm in."

Chase scowled, his jaws snapping together.

"I'm in, too," Willow said drawing instant ire from Josh, who paced the linoleum floor muttering under his breath.

Everyone had turned to Peyton but she was ready. "I'm in. This might be our only chance."

Ellis turned and strode out of the kitchen, and her heart sank as he disappeared around the corner. She couldn't turn her back on this opportunity, even if it meant turning away from the man she was falling in love with.

She picked up the wine bottle and refilled their glasses. They were going to need it.

"Now, what's the plan?"

Chapter Eighteen

THE PLAN WAS risky but worth a try. None of the men wanted the women out of their sight, so at about midnight when they were all cranky and exhausted from arguing about it, Peyton had thrown up her hands in frustration.

"Just come along with us," she said, rubbing her forehead and yawning. "What's the worst thing that can happen? They won't let you in and you wait outside the gate for us."

That was enough of a compromise to let them move forward. There were plans and contingency plans, and emergency plans but it all boiled down to one fact.

This was a huge risk and they could all end up dead.

Despite the danger hanging over her head, Peyton had managed to get some sleep but had awoken early just as the first bars of morning sun filtered through the curtains. Pulling on a pair of shorts and a t-shirt, she softly crept into the living room to see Ellis on the couch still asleep, a rare occurrence. Once he smelled the coffee, though, he'd be wide awake.

She was sipping her first cup when he joined in her in the kitchen, his dark hair delightfully rumpled. "It's not often you beat me out of bed."

"You were exhausted last night, not just from the activities of the day but from arguing with me for five hours. Chase and Josh gave up at three and a half."

He sat down at the table, his large hands dwarfing the mug. "I have more stamina."

"We have to do this."

He groaned and rubbed the stubble on his face. "I haven't had enough caffeine to shoot down that argument, princess. But I did do some thinking after everyone went to bed and you're right."

Scalding coffee burned her tongue. "Did you just say that I'm right? I cannot have heard you correctly."

"Haha, very funny. You're right in that we have to make something happen. We've lost momentum and we're spinning our wheels. Do we need to march into the lion's den like six walking T-bone steaks? Not necessarily."

"I'm open to better ideas."

His shoulders slumped. "I don't have any. As a cop the only thing I know to do is go back and start at the beginning. Go over the evidence and see if there's something we missed. I think we should do that anyway, no matter what happens tonight."

"I agree, but Nigel has had the opportunity to kill us and he didn't do it. Why would he wait until now?"

It was as if what she'd said had electrified him. He was fidgeting in his chair, his feet and hands moving nervously.

"It's funny you should mention that. This entire case has me twisted into knots. It's something else I was thinking about last night. Something that's been bugging me for days. For a world class organization with basically unlimited resources they are lousy at covert operations. Just terrible. They suck. Think about that for a moment." He hopped up from his chair, pacing the small space. "They tried to bug your homes but we found them. They tried to kill Holmwood. They failed. They tried to kill Hollister. Another failure and they failed to hurt us along with that. We were slowed down by some traffic that night. A cop car and a firetruck blocked the lanes but when we got up to them there wasn't any accident that I could see."

"Are you saying that it was planned?"

He stopped and whirled around to face her. "I think I'm losing my mind. It might have been one great big coincidence but I thought we didn't believe in those anymore. Listen to me, they haven't done one thing right. They let Josh waltz into The Clubhouse and look for files. They chased us down a London street and let us get away. They tried to break into Josh and Chase's house but were chased away by the dogs. This is not the work of a super secretive society that will do anything or kill anyone for power. In my experience, even terrible criminals get it right every now and then, if only by accident."

Her heart was pounding as his words penetrated her sleep-sluggish brain. "You think someone was protecting us?"

He shook his head. "No, princess, I think someone was *manipulating* us. Now that is what Evandria is good at. Making one thing look like something completely different. We've been so busy running and hiding we haven't concentrated on the real task. Finding who has the power and bringing them down."

Ellis was a smart cop and he just might be right. When looked at individually, each of the events didn't seem all that strange but when she looked at them all together, he had a point.

Evandria was terrible at killing people. But...

"Archer managed to kill our husbands," she pointed out. "They got that part right. They almost killed me."

"He did," Ellis agreed, sitting down again. "But that was five years ago and it was all about Arsenal. As for your injuries, the operative word is *almost*. You were almost killed but you weren't. For all we know they may have just wanted to scare us, not hurt you. The only reason you were near that package bomb is because you stopped to take a phone call. I'm honestly starting to believe that Evandria doesn't truly sees us as a threat to their power structure. We think we've been making progress but what if it was what they wanted all along? And this trial is the same? Get you three in there, do their dog and pony show, and send you on your way with assurances you'll be safe now."

Peyton licked her suddenly dry lips. "Then we've been pawns all along. They wanted us to dig up certain bodies so they didn't have to."

Her head hurt just thinking about it.

"Whoever *they* are. Is it the rogue faction? Is it the good guys? Are they one and the same? But yes, I think we've been used and I think Nigel Holmwood may have had a lot to do with that. Maybe even Grant Hollister and your brother and father too."

She wouldn't put anything past her father or Jensen. "Then maybe we shouldn't go tonight. Wouldn't that be playing into their hands?"

"I'm guessing they'll find another way to get us where they want. Maybe if we go in with our eyes open, we can get the upper hand for once."

All the running and hiding. All the research. Her coma. Finding out the secrets Greg had carried to the grave. All of it. None of it had made a bit of difference.

"We were never one step ahead, were we?" she asked sadly, her gaze meeting Ellis's.

"I don't think so. I think they've played us every step of the way."

"What about our meeting? Was that an accident too?"

Both Peyton and Ellis turned to see Willow standing in the doorway, tears glistening in her eyes.

Ellis glanced at Peyton before answering. "No, I don't think it was. I think the three of you were supposed to meet. If not that evening, then some other one. I think that fire in the kitchen that first night was set deliberately to force you out into that parking lot where you might run into each other."

Just like that, everything was different.

Chapter Nineteen

ELLIS HAD BEEN expecting trouble at the gates of Evandria but the guard hadn't blinked an eye at his and Josh's presence with the women. Chase had stayed behind in what they were calling a "just in case" move. Ellis had given his friend the name of his FBI buddy since contacting the local police would likely be a waste of time.

If they didn't come out of the compound by morning, Chase was to call in the Feds, but Ellis doubted they were going to need to do anything rash. The more he thought about his theory, the more he believed it. Whether the women were truly in danger he didn't know, but he didn't have that feeling of foreboding in his gut anymore. There was anger, chewing away at him like acid, but the heart-stopping fear for Peyton's life had been tempered. Evandria was playing a game with them and Ellis needed to figure out the goddamn rules as soon as possible.

The guard had directed him to The Clubhouse and Ellis pulled the vehicle into a parking space as Nigel Holmwood strode out the back entrance where Josh had snuck in.

"Remember, we're here to listen and take in as much information as possible," Ellis said as they exited the car. "Let's look at things from the perspective of what they get out of our presence, not how it helps us."

"Bailey, darling, it's so good to see you." Holmwood embraced her. "I'll be taking you in this back door to an observation area. I would ask that you not speak to any members or employees except for me while you're in the building. Your being here is quite controversial and we're only revealing it to a few select members. You may, of course, speak to one another."

"The officers?" Josh asked as they followed him into the building. "I assume they know."

"A few."

Ellis and Josh exchanged a glance that spoke volumes between them. Holmwood was definitely playing a game with them and perhaps all the other officers.

To Ellis's surprise the elevator took them down. To have a "basement" in Florida, the building had to have been built "up" in elevation so that what appeared to be the first floor was actually the second. The doors slid open and Holmwood ushered them down an ornate hallway with thick carpets on the floor and heavy oak furniture. Paintings of famous people – who must have also been members – hung on the walls. At one point, there was a picture of the US Congress chambers with little flags on certain seats both left and right of the aisle. It looked like Evandria didn't care if a person was Republican or Democrat.

He opened a door near the end of the hall and waited while they filed in. The room wasn't large but it was comfortable with several chairs and two small sofas arranged facing one wall covered in a floor to ceiling blood red curtain.

"Please make yourselves comfortable. There are refreshments at the bar." He pointed to one side of the room before picking up a small woven basket on the table by the door. "I would ask that you turn off your cell phones and place them here. I won't be taking them with me but this way you won't be tempted to use them. These proceedings are absolutely secret. I'm afraid this is mandatory if you wish to remain. If you're unwilling to part with your phones I can have you escorted to the Resort where you can wait for your friends."

The last thing Ellis wanted to give up was his phone but he had little choice if he wanted to stay. Powering the device down, he tossed it in the basket along with everyone else.

"Thank you," Nigel smiled. "They'll be here by the door and you can pick them up on the way out. I appreciate your cooperation. Evandria has many quirks but they've worked for us through the years. Now, do you have any questions?"

Loads. Where did he begin?

Willow was the first to speak. "Where have you been keeping Archer? Do you have some sort of prison here?"

If Holmwood was surprised by the question, he hid it well. "A prison isn't necessary. He's been kept in a secured area of the Retreat with his every move monitored. He is well aware that he wouldn't leave this property alive."

"Who all is invited to something like this?" Peyton asked. She had to be thinking about her father and whether he would attend or if she might run into him here.

Nigel walked over to the heavy red curtain and pulled it back, revealing a room on the other side of a large window. Tables set up in a circle ringed a single chair in the center.

People were beginning to enter and sit down. Ellis recognized two senators and the CEO of a Wall Street firm that he'd seen interviewed on television.

"No one can see you. From that room, this window looks like a mirror. As for who is attending, you can see for yourself. These are Evandria's officers." He pointed to the rows of chairs off to the side. "Those are for senior members who were once officers. The answer to your unspoken question, Peyton, is yes. Your father will be attending today's trial. Your brother Jensen will not. He is not someone you should trust."

Ellis was fucking tired of this shit. "Because?"

Nigel turned to him and nodded. "Jensen cannot be trusted to speak the truth."

"We figured that out without your help," Ellis groused. "What we need to know is why. Why can't Peyton trust Jensen? What has he done?"

"It's not for me to say."

"Why not?" Ellis asked sharply. "I think I speak for all of us when I say that we're getting damn tired of you speaking in riddles. Just fucking say what you mean."

The old man appeared completely unperturbed by Ellis's vitriol, which in of itself was suspicious. "When I say Jensen or someone else cannot be trusted I often cannot give you specifics. I may have suspicions but nothing concrete."

"So this is your gut talking?" Peyton cut in. "You just *think* I can't trust my brother? But you don't know anything for sure?"

"Precisely. I would hate to see you hurt if you did trust him."

Willow crossed her arms over her chest and tapped her foot on the plush carpeting. "So whom can we trust? Is there a list?"

Holmwood smiled. "You can trust me."

"Convenient," remarked Josh, strolling over to the large observation window and pointing to Grant Hollister who had just sat down at a table. "Grant says we shouldn't trust you."

"And yet I was the one who brought you here," Holmwood said. "Not Hollister. Ask yourself why."

Chuckling, Ellis joined Josh by the window. "Funny you should mention that. I have been doing a lot of thinking these past few days and I think I may have come to the conclusion that we're doing your dirty work for you. We take all the risks and you get what you've always wanted. Archer Caldwell on trial. Am I close?"

Holmwood smiled. "I find that people will believe whatever they want to, so it would be foolish of me to try and change your mind. Now if you will excuse me, I have duties elsewhere. Please remember the rules. You must stay in this room the entire time and you must not talk to anyone but me. Do you understand?"

"Uncle Nigel," Bailey said before he was able to leave the room. "I do have one more question. Is that okay?"

"Of course, my dear. What is it?"

She pointed across the room they were observing where a large mirror hung on the wall.

"Who is in that room on the other side?"

"VIP guests. Members whose families go back to the founding of Evandria. Now I do have to go. I'll see you when it's over."

Holmwood slipped out of the room, leaving the five of them alone. Or as alone as one could be in Evandria. The room was in probability bugged for sound and maybe even videoed as well.

Ellis headed straight for the bar with Josh on his heels. They could all use a drink.

"There's my father." Peyton's face was pressed up against the glass. "I guess Nigel was telling the truth about that."

"That's probably all he was telling the truth about." Josh accepted a high ball glass of whiskey from Ellis. "I don't care what he says. I don't trust him."

"He's always told us the truth," Bailey protested. "He's never lied to us."

Rolling her eyes, Willow tossed back a gulp of the amber liquid. "Come on, he's lied to you for years. He lied about Evandria. He lied about Arsenal and Frank. He lied about his lies. He's a big, fat liar and he's brought us here for a reason and it's not out of the goodness of his heart. If we're not careful we'll find ourselves implicated in our husbands' murders."

"Don't give them any ideas," Peyton shuddered. "I'm not sure whether I should trust Jensen but I'm sure I don't trust Nigel."

Lips pressed into a thin line, Bailey picked up her whiskey glass. "Who are we supposed to trust? Grant? He almost got us killed that night at Roy's."

"He's done nothing but try to help us," Willow protested. "He's the reason we're even here today for Archer's trial. Without him we'd still be searching for the truth."

While the women argued, Ellis had wandered over to the window to study the scene laid out before him. The tables were inhabited by roughly the same amount of women as men, with many recognizable faces including Hollister's. But the thing that had Ellis's real attention was the VIP gallery Bailey had asked about.

Just who did that include?

"We can't trust anyone," Ellis said without bothering to turn around. Bickering wasn't going to solve this problem. It didn't change the facts, of which they had few. Paranoia? Conjecture? They had those in spades. "Trust no one but each other. That's it. Everyone else is suspect even if they've told us the truth in the past."

Josh smiled, chuckling softly. "That makes the math easy."

Ellis lifted his glass in salute. "I try to help when I can."

Peyton nodded toward the window. "I think they're starting."

Everyone in the room had taken a seat and two burly men were escorting Archer Caldwell to the chair in the center.

It had begun.

Chapter Twenty

T HE ROOM WAS quiet as were Peyton, Ellis, and their friends. Archer Caldwell was as well-dressed as any of the officers or observers in a dark blue bespoke suit. If she hadn't known he was the defendant she would have mistaken him for one of the members. He looked like the businessman that he was, not a serial killer, which he'd proven to be also.

Nigel had taken a seat at what appeared to be the head table next to an older well-dressed woman wearing a dark pantsuit and short blonde hair. She looked familiar but Peyton couldn't place her. Perhaps she'd seen her at one of her parents' parties over the years or maybe she'd seen her on television.

Out of the corner of her eye she watched her father as he sat in the gallery, looking stately and superior in his gray pin-striped suit. When he'd walked in he'd been leaning on his gold-handled cane which told her that his bad knee was bothering him. After too much golf and some wet weather he always ended up complaining about his knee.

The woman stood, a stoic and serious expression on her face. "We are here today to hear serious charges against an Evandrian brother, Archer William Caldwell. These allegations are egregious, and because of that we must be sure when we render our verdict today. But once we do…" The woman paused for effect. "If found guilty, justice must be swift and sure. But if innocent, we must as a family move on from this and find a way to work together. The mission of Evandria is more important than any petty arguments between our members. Now may we have the reading of the charges?"

Nigel stood, thanked the woman quietly and read from a paper sitting on the table.

"Today we come before you to accuse Archer Caldwell of not one…not two…but three murders of our own Evandria brothers. Frank Scott, Alex Vaughn, and Greg Nelson would be here today if not for his treachery against his own family."

Peyton released the breath she'd been holding as Nigel sat down again, taking off his glasses and setting them next to a glass of water. The woman picked up a gavel – she was apparently the judge – and pounded it once on the table.

"Who is the accuser?"

Grant Hollister stood and nodded to the attendees. "I am."

"You will act as prosecutor today?"

"I will."

Willow had leaned forward in her chair to get a better view of her half-brother-in-law with Josh resting his hand on her shoulder. Everyone was on the edge of their seats.

"Does the accused have a defender?"

Archer stood. "I am defending myself."

Fool. Was there no one who would take his side?

The woman looked down at the stack of papers in front of

her. "Then a defender will be appointed for you." She leaned closer to Holmwood and they spoke for a moment. "Charles McMillen, you have been chosen."

Peyton stiffened in shock as her father nodded and slowly stood, hobbling to the lone empty chair in the circle.

"Nigel knows I'm sitting back here," she said quietly but loud enough to be heard. "He did that on purpose. My father against Alex's half-brother."

Even Bailey couldn't defend her uncle on this act, and Ellis had tensed up next to Peyton, his anger clearly written in his expression. It was a good thing Nigel was in another room because Ellis would have decked him.

"He's just playing with us," he murmured. "This is all just a game to him."

Grant stood and outlined the charges again, playing the recording they'd all heard regarding Greg's death. Strangely, no one mentioned Jensen or that he should be called to testify afterward. It was as if his name had never been spoken aloud. Peyton had scrutinized her father closely while the recording was playing, looking for any sort of reaction but she was disappointed. He remained silent and stoic the entire time. Perhaps Jensen had been telling the truth and the recording was referring to someone else.

Peyton's father stood, leaning on his cane, and questioned the veracity of the recording and citing technology as a possibility of how it had come to be. She was pretty sure no one bought that argument but it wasn't a bad one.

Charles McMillen still didn't mention Jensen's name, instead just listening with a neutral expression. She'd seen him look the same when he watched the evening news.

Then Grant presented Archer's own confession which had been videotaped. Peyton didn't learn anything new from it, but it corroborated the confession that Willow and Josh heard at the car warehouse.

Grant sat down. "The prosecution rests."

The judge raised the gavel and brought it down. "A ten-minute recess and we'll resume."

"That's it?" Josh asked, stepping back from the window. "All he has to do is say that confession was coerced and he walks out of here a free man."

Feeling sick to her stomach, Peyton sought out Ellis sitting next to her for some sort of optimism but he didn't look any happier than his friends. "Do you think what Josh said is true?"

"It's a possibility," Ellis replied grimly. "If this were a regular court of law he'd have a decent shot at a not guilty verdict or maybe even have the charges dismissed. It all depends on the judge, frankly. I don't suppose your father went to law school?"

Peyton shook her head. "He's a businessman but maybe he watched 'Perry Mason'."

Willow groaned. "Don't even say that. All we need is a surprise witness no one has ever heard of. He's already confessed. That should be enough."

Was it enough? If Archer was in the real justice system, the case probably never would have come to trial. His money could buy him the best defense in the world, after all. But apparently not in the Evandria world. Her father had been pressed into service, although he didn't look upset about it.

Ellis refilled everyone's glasses as the trial started again. Her father stood next to Archer, who had taken the seat in the middle of the room once more.

"Archer Caldwell." Her father's voice boomed in the silence. "Did you have anything to do with the murders of Frank Scott, Alex Vaughn, and Greg Nelson?"

Caldwell nodded. "I did."

Not even a peep from the crowd. They were either unsurprised or well-trained.

"For what reason did you involve yourself in their killings?"

Lifting his chin, Archer smiled. "I was under orders from senior Evandria officers."

That had the crowd murmuring until the judge used her gavel, quieting them down.

Charles McMillen continued. "So it is your testimony that you killed these three brothers because you received a lawful order?"

Grant stood immediately. "May we define lawful order?"

"Any order from a senior officer is consider lawful, Mr. Hollister," her father replied. "It's in the bylaws."

Grant's jaw tightened. "For the order to be lawful it must be entered into record. What senior officer gave this order?"

"I cannot say," Caldwell answered.

The judge sat forward in her seat. "Cannot or will not?"

Archer's face was impassive. "I don't see that it matters either way. I killed three men. If you believe I was following a lawful order, then I'm innocent. If not, I'm guilty. No more of these games. Just vote."

"You are entitled to a defense," the judge argued. "Would you like more time?"

"No."

The silence stretched and Peyton barely took a breath as the judge weighed her options. Finally she brought down her gavel, the sound echoing in the large room.

"Time to vote."

"What will happen?" Bailey whispered, although no one in the other room could hear them. "Are they going to let him go on a technicality?"

Standing, Ellis scraped his fingers through his hair, his blue eyes almost silver with suppressed emotion. "I have no idea what they're going to do in there or if he even has any allies in the organization. When he said he was going to defend himself I thought this would be a cakewalk but now…"

Peyton had thought the same thing, but then Nigel Holmwood had dragged her father into this farce just to be an asshole. He thought it was funny to pit the women against each other but they weren't that petty. If Grant didn't prevail, Willow and Bailey weren't going to hold it against Peyton. Nigel didn't understand the people he was trying to manipulate.

The voting was more fascinating than the testimony portion. Each officer had three small balls in front of them – one red, one white, and one black. One of the observers went to each officer, stood in front of the table, and held out two bags, one blue and one green. The officer would place one of the balls in the blue velvet bag, and the other two balls were dropped into the green bag.

An anonymous vote.

"What does each ball color mean?" Willow asked, moving to get a better angle. "There's three so maybe it's guilty, not guilty, can't decide."

When everyone had voted, the man placed the blue velvet bag in front of the judge. She spoke briefly to Nigel before opening the bag and separating them by color in three bowls sitting in front of her. Peyton's attention must have been somewhere else because they hadn't been there mere moments before. It didn't take long to see the decision.

There were about six white balls.

About six black balls.

And about ten or more red balls.

Red had won the vote, whatever that meant. Unless it had to be unanimous. Would it then be a mistrial? Would Archer walk free?

The woman judge rose to her feet. "The voting is as follows. Six votes for not guilty. Seven votes for guilty and blackballing the member. Eleven votes for guilty and punishment. Archer Caldwell, do you understand the verdict that has been rendered on this day?"

"I do."

Caldwell smirked as he replied to the judge, clearly not too upset about the verdict. Maybe punishment meant he had to mow lawns or wash cars. He hadn't been expelled from the group, which blackballing would have done. He was still part of Evandria even after being found guilty of three murders.

"Nice group they have here," Willow fumed. "He gets some sort of punishment and that's it. That's bullshit."

Acid had risen in the back of Peyton's throat and she had to swallow hard to keep her whiskey from coming back up. "I know this sounds lame but whatever he gets from Evandria is more than he would have gotten in the regular justice system. Nothing would have happened to him there."

Bailey's eyes were bright with tears. "You have a point. At least he admitted to it and everyone knows. That has to count for something."

Willow's cheeks were wet. "It doesn't count for shit. This was a waste of our time. We learned nothing."

Ellis shook his head, his gaze trained on the room where the members were leaving a few at a time. Archer Caldwell had already been removed. "We learned that their justice system isn't much better than ours."

Josh wrapped his arm around Willow's shoulders. "It was a kangaroo court. How much do you want to bet the outcome was already decided before we ever stepped foot in this building?"

Chase knocked back the last of his whiskey. "Archer was loyal though. He didn't snitch on who gave him the order. That was the name we really needed."

The door opened and Nigel Holmwood walked into the room, stopping abruptly when he faced six hostile occupants. Frowning, he gazed at them in confusion.

"Aren't you happy with the results? It was better than I ever hoped for."

"That's a good result?" Willow asked bitterly. "It's pathetic, is what it is."

"You didn't think he should be found guilty?" Holmwood asked, his brows pulled down.

Bailey stood and moved toward him. "I think we were hoping for something more than just a simple punishment, Uncle Nigel. At least with the blackball he would lose his Evandria membership but with the red he gets to stay a member."

Holmwood blinked a few times and then his expression relaxed. "Children, you don't understand and I blame myself for that. I should have explained it before I left you but I was in such a hurry. White means not guilty. Black means guilty and he would be banished from the organization. Red, however, is more serious than black and frankly I didn't think we'd get it because of his argument about a lawful order. That was a gray area I didn't expect."

Placing his hands on her shoulders, Ellis stood behind Peyton. "Then what does red mean?"

"Red is the death penalty."

Chapter Twenty-One

PEYTON AND ELLIS didn't say much as they drove back to the safe house. He wasn't rendered speechless often but Holmwood had managed to do it when he'd declared that Archer Caldwell would face the death penalty. Ellis hadn't been expecting that.

It was around midnight when they all wearily entered the house, yawning and stretching. Bailey and Willow headed straight for the kitchen but Peyton took a right turn down the hall to her bedroom. If she wanted to be alone, he could respect that.

He walked outside, the air damp at this time of night, and looked up at the stars. It was a little something he did when he started getting too wrapped up in his day job, thinking that the fate of the world hung on his every decision.

He just wasn't that important. Staring up at the wide expanse of sky served to remind him that he was but one small speck on an enormous planet. In the big scheme of things, what he did or didn't do wasn't all that big a deal. He needed that reminder today. While he'd helped find Peyton's husband's killer, the real person responsible was still unknown, presuming that Caldwell was even telling the truth. He'd hoped for so much more but he didn't know how to make that happen. He had to face the reality that he might not be able to help Peyton and her friends.

"You spending the night out here?" Chase asked, appearing at Ellis's elbow. "You'll be eaten alive by mosquitos."

"I wish I still smoked."

Chuckling, Chase sat down on the old swing on the back porch. "Because the smoke would scare away the bugs?"

Ellis tore his gaze away from the stars and over to his friend. "Because I could really use a cigarette. They used to calm me."

"Nicotine is a stimulant, my friend, and for your information it did not used to calm you. Not at all. You were the same grouchy asshole you always were."

"With friends like you..."

Ellis didn't need to finish his sentence, and Chase laughed anyway. "Want to tell me what you're doing out here? It's not like there's a cool breeze or anything. It's hot and humid even in the middle of the damn night."

"Welcome to Florida."

Chase stretched out his legs. "I told Bailey I'd move down here and I will, but this summer weather is something else. Hotter than Hades and it rains every day at the same time."

"What if we couldn't keep them safe?" Ellis asked abruptly. "What would you do then?"

Chase levered up from the swing and came over to the porch railing where Ellis stood.

"Josh and I talked about that some."

"And?"

Silence except for the crickets and the cicadas.

"Why don't you tell me what you were thinking?" Chase asked instead. "You're the cop."

"You're the genius," Ellis shot back. "You're supposed to be smarter than me."

"Not when it comes to hiding and running. So tell me, what were you thinking?"

"Going under," Ellis admitted quietly. "A new name and a new life. If we couldn't bring them down it seemed like the only option. Crazy, huh?"

"Not so insane since Josh and I had that same idea pass through our skulls as well. But I thought you don't think Evandria is all that dangerous. You said they were manipulating us, but you don't think they're deadly."

Those would be famous last words to carve on his tombstone. "What if I'm wrong? It's a theory, Chase, and not much more than that. What if we leave this safe house and one of them gets hurt or killed? What if this goes on and on and on? I don't think these ladies are cut out for a life on the run. Are you?"

Chase sighed. "I don't think any of us know how we would react to that. I know one thing though. This is not just your fight. You're putting way too much pressure on yourself and it's not healthy. We're all in this together. I know you love her, but she's not going to turn away from you if you can't bring down Evandria."

That was it. Right there. His fear that he'd been unable to vocalize. They'd only just begun their relationship. It could fall apart so easily.

"It's all I have to offer."

The raw words seemed to come from somewhere deep inside of him and Chase seemed to understand their meaning.

"That's not true. Not true at all."

"You have money—"

Chase didn't even let Ellis finish. "Don't do this. Peyton doesn't care about your money or lack thereof. She doesn't care about what you think you bring to the relationship. All she cares about is someone that loves and respects her. Shit, that's what all three of them want after what they've been through. They've had the money and the glamour and it didn't make them happy. They want the love and you can deliver that."

"I don't think you believed that a few weeks ago."

Laughing, Chase slapped Ellis on the back. "What can I say? I'm a complicated man. But let me tell you what I've seen since you met Peyton. I've seen a man dedicated to keeping a woman safe whether he gained anything from it or not. Not many men would do that."

"Not many men are as stupid as I am," Ellis mocked.

"You got that right. None of us are very bright but we make up for it in looks. Now go in there and talk to your woman. She was upset earlier."

"And wanted to be alone."

Chase turned to go back inside. "Since when do you give a shit what other people want?"

Good point. Ellis followed his friend into the house. Time to see how Peyton was doing.

"COME IN," PEYTON called when she heard the knock on her bedroom door. It was Ellis, of course. He'd left her alone far longer than she'd thought he would. Long enough, in fact, that she'd dozed off lying on the bed still fully clothed.

"There's food in the kitchen if you're hungry."

She shook her head. He was always worried about whether she'd eaten or not. It was one of the ways he showed he cared. "I don't think my stomach can handle food right now. Did you eat?"

He held up an apple. "Grabbed one as I walked through the kitchen. Bailey made a frozen pizza though."

"Absolutely not."

Scooting over on the mattress to make room, Peyton settled back on a stack of pillows.

"Do you want to talk about it?" he eventually asked after the silence stretched on for a long time. "Or do you want me to leave you alone?"

Sometimes he didn't have a clue. "I definitely do not want you to leave me alone. I came in here thinking you would follow me."

"I thought you wanted to be by yourself for awhile. You had that look on your face." He tugged on one of her pillows. "I don't suppose I can have one of these? My pillow is in the living room."

She lifted up and let him pull out one from the stack. "Because you've been sleeping on the couch. When you sleep, that is."

"You'd be surprised how comfortable that forty-year-old couch is."

She giggled, batting her hand at his arm as she stared up at the ceiling. "I would be shocked plus it smells a little musty."

"Didn't notice."

"Liar."

He rolled to his side so he was lying next to her, his arm brushing hers. "So what if I did? There are only three bedrooms in this house. I'm lucky I'm not sleeping in the car. Which, by the way, I've done several times in my job so it wouldn't be a big deal."

Three bedrooms. Bailey and Chase in one. Willow and Josh in the second. Peyton in the third. Willow had pulled Peyton aside earlier today and expressed surprise that Ellis had slept on the couch. That even if they weren't *sleeping together*, they could...sleep together.

Peyton knew better. If she had Ellis in her bed she wasn't going to waste time with sleep. She'd been celibate a long time and for all the right reasons. Too old for casual sex. Wanting something more than what she'd had with Greg. Their sex life had not been good and he hadn't been shy about letting her know.

Now she had a good man and it wouldn't be a one-night thing. This was a real relationship with emotions and feelings and...desire. She wanted him and she'd been playing it safe for far too long. What had happened to that free-spirited young girl she once was that had been determined to live her life by her own rules? She wouldn't have made Ellis sleep on the couch.

Peyton had become a person she barely recognized during her marriage but she was finally coming out of her self-imposed cocoon.

"You should sleep here tonight."

Damn poker face. His expression didn't even flicker at her words that had to have come as a shock to him. Or was he doing that "Ellis thing" again where he knew her wants and needs better than she knew herself. He seemed to have an uncanny ability to anticipate her needs when she was recovering in the hospital. Out in the real world she hadn't encouraged that behavior.

"I could do that."

He was making her nervous. Did he not want to? She'd assumed he'd jump at the chance.

"You know, if you want to."

"I want to."

Slapping the comforter, she sat up. "You could look a little happy about it or something."

"I am happy."

He was playing with her but she couldn't stop herself from falling for it every time. She shoved his shoulder, her lips pressed tightly together. "I've seen happier mourners at a funeral."

He captured her hand and brought it to his lips. "Peyton, I am happy. I am also afraid that you will change your mind so I am staying very still and trying not to make any sudden moves just in case you get spooked."

Oh. That made sense. She'd run him ragged getting to this point.

"I'm not going to change my mind."

This time it was his turn to sit up. "You say that…"

Kneeling on the mattress, she pressed her lips to his trying to put everything she was having trouble saying into that kiss, hoping he would get the message.

"I want this," she said when they broke apart. "I want us. For the first time in a long time I'm ready to be happy. After the trial today, I realized that we actually accomplished something. Greg's killer is going to pay for his crimes, and he had to answer for what he did in front of his friends and peers. That's something and since we may never figure out who put him up to him, I have to be happy about that."

Peyton didn't think she'd ever get used to how handsome Ellis was when he smiled. "So this is for real?"

"If you want it to be."

"That's what I've wanted since the moment I met you."

He was holding back. She could feel it, the energy he kept under iron control. If she had to be blunt then that's what she'd do.

"Ellis, it's time." She reached for the hem of his t-shirt and tugged it up, exposing the golden flesh of his torso. "A little cooperation would be nice."

But she'd do all the work if she had to.

Chapter Twenty-Two

THIS WAS AN Ellis she hadn't expected. An intense man out of bed, she'd assumed he'd be the same under the covers. Much to her amazement, he was much more playful than brooding. Tickling here, nibbling there. Whispering rather naughty suggestions in her ear. It was an empowering feeling, seeing how happy and carefree he acted when they were together like this.

He'd stripped her of her sundress and panties quickly but he still had his pants on and they needed to go. Her fingers brushed the zipper and his hips bucked, drawing a sharp breath from his lips. Popping open the top button, she tugged down the zipper and then shimmied the trousers down his muscular thighs before tossing them aside. Ellis was now lounging against the pillows, his gaze following her every move which only served to make undressing him much hotter and arousing.

Her next goal was his tented boxers but his strong hands captured her wrists, kissing each palm before she could reach them.

"Are you sure? Because once you let him out of his cage..."

Giggling, she leaned down and pressed kisses down his treasure trail, making him move restlessly under her. "Tell me you didn't name it."

"He doesn't have a name but he is definitely not an *it*. Have a little respect, princess."

This glowering, grouchy man was *fun*. Thank goodness she'd given them a chance because missing out on this would have been tragic.

"Should I call him sir?"

He took her hand and placed it on the fabric covering his extremely hard cock and her hand reflexively tightened around it. "Baby, I bet he'll let you call him whatever you want, but his favorite names are *harder* and *faster*."

No longer able to keep a straight face, she laid down next to him laughing so hard tears began to leak from her eyes. In her experience sex was something serious and giggling was not allowed, but it was so much better with a little levity. "Have you used these lines on women and do they work?"

He rolled over, his rough fingers pinching a nipple until it was hard and erect and she was breathless and reeling. "I have used them and I can say unequivocally they do not work at all. But they are funny and they break the ice."

Ellis was trying to make her more comfortable, not wanting her to be nervous. It was working.

Peyton ran her hands up his muscled torso and over his wide shoulders, feeling every ridge and plane of his body. The hair on his arms and legs was slightly rougher than her own, the skin hotter under her palms. It was the sprinkling of light brown hair on his chest that had her fascinated. It was silky and fine when she carded her fingers through it, tickling her flesh.

His own hands had claimed the territory north of her belly button and was exploring every sensitive inch until she was panting for more. Her heart beat heavily against her ribs as blood pulsed though her veins all the way to the tips of her fingers and toes. Burying his face in her neck, she could feel him take a deep inhale of her scent before he nibbled and licked at the sensitive spot behind her ear. She'd have a love bite there tomorrow but tonight she didn't care. It all felt too good and any thought of editing his actions was long gone.

His breath tickled her skin as he kissed a wet trail down her neck, chest, and over her quivering abdomen, stopping only for a moment to place kisses on the pink tips of her breasts. His tongue dipped into her belly button for a second before painting swirls all the way to her hipbone. Her hips canted and her fingers dug into his shoulders at the rioting sensations he'd evoked with so little effort.

"Ellis," she sighed as his warm breath caressed that most intimate place. Perhaps she should have been self-conscious or shy but the heated glances he'd been giving her didn't leave room for modesty and hesitation. This man accepted all of her and he'd seen her at her worst, his desire never once faltering. Their relationship was more than whether her stomach was flat or whether his hair was receding. She'd feel this way when he was seventy and bald.

She wriggled at the first touch of his tongue, tracing her seam before he delved in, lapping at her clit. Peyton whimpered as her temperature rose and flames swept over her flesh. She crumpled the sheets in her tight fists and her lids fluttered shut, suddenly too heavy to hold open. Insinuating himself between her thighs, he pushed her legs farther apart as his large hands gripped her hips, holding her in place. His talented and wicked tongue gave her no respite as he teased and played, giving and taking in equal measures and holding her on the edge, her legs trembling.

It was only when he pressed two fingers inside her soaked channel that she went over, her entire being dissolving with pleasure. White light burned behind her lids as everything but the two of them fell away, her world narrowing to him, this bed, and the way he could make her feel. By the time she reluctantly returned to reality he had crawled up her body and was hovering above her. His large body dwarfed her own, making her feel small, delicate, and incredibly protected.

"Princess?"

Blinking to clear her still fuzzy vision, she took a deep breath and smiled. "It's all good. Trust me. Very good. Good."

He'd short-circuited her brain and putting full sentences together was impossible, but he seemed to understand. Dipping his head down, he took a sensitive nipple into his mouth and worried it with his lips and teeth, starting her journey to the precipice once more. Not wanting to neglect the other side, he plucked at the other with his fingers until she was moving restlessly under him, ready for the next part. Ready for him. Her thigh brushed his hard cock and he groaned, his mouth tightening on an already taut peak.

He pulled away and a gust of cool air ran over her overheated flesh, sending goosebumps up and down her arms and making her shiver. She'd opened her mouth to protest but he was back, holding up a foil packet. At least one of them had enough of their wits about them to be practical. He'd pushed everything out of her mind but him.

Ripping it open with his teeth, he was about to roll it on but her own hand stayed his movements. This first time had been fast and heated so far, and she'd barely been able to explore. Although she knew there would be many chances in the future, she needed to touch him. Now.

"Let me."

"Yes, ma'am," he said huskily, his voice deep and rough. He surrendered the condom to her and she rolled it on him, taking her time and making sure her fingers caressed every steely inch.

When it was on she didn't let go, instead guiding him exactly where she wanted him. Peyton wanted there to be no question between them tonight. There would be no morning recriminations, no afterthoughts. She wanted this, was eager for it, and there wouldn't be a doubt in either of their minds.

He brushed at her slit, slick and ready for him, pushing forward slightly and then pulling back. On the next stroke he thrust in farther, pushing the oxygen from her lungs, before once again retreating. Her hands wrapped around his biceps and she pressed her lips to every part of him that she could reach: collarbone, neck, and chest, wanting to send a message of how much this meant to her.

I want you. I need you.

Finally he buried himself in to the hilt, her walls stretching to accommodate his generous size. A coil of arousal began forming in her abdomen as every inch of him filled every nook and cranny inside of her.

Closing her eyes, she forced herself to breathe in and out as her body grew accustomed to the feeling of being taken after so long. Their two bodies were joined in the most intimate of ways, and their breaths and heartbeats synchronized as their bodies seemed to meld together. She felt his exhale of relief on her shoulder when she experimentally moved her hips, swaying them from side to side. Her breath hitched as pleasure fizzed through her veins, sending her closer to completion.

Ellis started slowly at first but then faster as she wrapped her legs around his slim hips, urging him on, needing more. His breathing labored and ragged, his hips snapped with each thrust, his cock dragging over that sweet spot inside of her. She cried out his name as he reached between them to rub circles around her already sensitive clit. Shattering into a million pieces, she spun as stars whirled around her, making her dizzy with pleasure. Ellis went still above her, his head thrown back and the cords of his neck exposed, a picture of pure male beauty.

Collapsing, he rolled to his side, taking her with him so she was tucked into his chest, his chin resting on the top of her head. They didn't move for a long time as they got their breathing under control and their pulses slowed down. Eventually he rolled away and disposed of the condom but was back immediately, cuddling her close as the sweat dried on their skin. Wordlessly she traced patterns on his chest with her fingernail, content to enjoy the closeness. It was something she hadn't had in a long time, if ever. This easiness with another human being was addicting and she couldn't get enough of it.

But of course she couldn't keep quiet forever. Her chest felt too small for her heart, and she had so much she wanted to express to Ellis. In typical fashion, he'd created a safe place for her to do just that.

"There's love here," she said finally, pressing her forehead into his shoulder. "I feel different. Like it's changed me."

She felt rather than heard his chuckle rumbling through his chest. "It's changed me too. I kind of like it though."

She nodded. "Me too. I guess I just didn't think it would be like this."

His fingers ran through her tangled hair, his thumb brushing her ear. "Should I be brave and ask what you thought it would be like?"

"I thought it would be the same but it's not. It's bigger, better. More all-encompassing. I'm not afraid or worried about losing it. It's as if this has been waiting for me all my life and now that it's here, it's a part of me now. Does that make sense?"

She'd rambled a bit more but the explanation was the best she could do. Describing a feeling wasn't easy.

"It makes perfect sense," he assured her, dropping a kiss to her temple. "This love isn't going anywhere. You're stuck with me. I hope you thought this through because I'm helpless against it."

"You're the strongest man I know so that's hard to believe."

He lifted her chin so she was looking into those blue eyes, so soft and full of adoration.

"How about I don't want to fight it? I'm happy to lose this battle because I get you."

Letting Ellis in didn't mean she wasn't strong. It took courage to open up her heart one more time. Whatever happened after this with Evandria wasn't important. The only thing that mattered was her future with this man.

Chapter Twenty-Three

A S MUCH AS Ellis wished differently, reality was waiting for Peyton and himself the next morning. They couldn't hide under the covers and pretend the rest of the world didn't exist. Decisions had to be made regarding this fucked-up investigation. The case was stalled and they'd made no progress in days. They either needed to retrench or quit.

He wasn't a man that liked giving up but they could work on this for years and never get anywhere. His own supervisor who had put him on this case was getting impatient at the lack of concrete evidence and had been broadly hinting that perhaps it was time to come back. Ellis had been doing most of this on his "vacation" time but he was the official detective assigned to Peyton's attempted murder case. However, there were now other cases stacked up in his absence – homicides, burglaries, and more. As his time off dwindled, he faced the real possibility of having to take an extended leave, assuming it would even be approved.

He didn't say anything as he cooked breakfast for the group – this morning it was pancakes. When everybody had eaten he would gather them together and ask the question outright.

Did they want to keep going?

It wasn't an outrageous query. Josh needed desperately to get back to his veterinary practice and all of his dogs. Bailey had a business to run as well, although her manager had done an excellent job keeping things humming so far. Chase could do his trading from anywhere but he wasn't spending any time doing it from what Ellis could see, which meant his friend wasn't making any money. It didn't help that the tension level was so high that they were beginning to turn on each other.

"Ellis, come in here," Chase called from the living room. "Now."

Turning off the stove, Ellis joined his friends who were trying to watch the morning news on the old television. The picture wasn't that great but he could hear the reporter loud and clear.

"His body was found in his car early this morning by the housekeeper who immediately called 911. It was too late, however, for the wealthy philanthropist who had succumbed to what is believed to be carbon monoxide poisoning. Insiders say the death will be ruled a suicide. The community of Midnight Blue Beach will certainly miss Archer Caldwell. His tireless work on behalf of children was legendary in the area."

At some point Peyton had come to stand beside Ellis, her hand wrapped around his arm, clinging tightly. Her face had gone quite pale and she was visibly shaken by the news. He wasn't feeling all that terrific himself. They'd all heard what Nigel said last night but Ellis hadn't believed it. Not really. He'd assumed it was a verdict that wouldn't actually be carried out.

There would be appeal after appeal. Time would pass. People would forget. Caldwell would be confined to The Retreat and that would be it. The end of the story.

Chase switched off the television. "I'm not sure how much you heard. They found him in the driver's seat of his car parked in the garage with the door down. I doubt he lasted long."

Breakfast forgotten, Ellis sat down heavily into the cushions of the couch. "Do you think they forced him? Tied up him up?"

Josh shook his head. "They didn't say anything about foul play and they think it's a suicide. Maybe they gave Caldwell a choice. Do it himself or they'd do it for him."

"They didn't waste any time," Peyton said faintly, coming to sit beside Ellis. "I'm stunned. When Nigel said he got the death penalty I never thought…"

Ellis put his arm around her shoulders, pulling her close. "Neither did I."

Josh hopped to his feet, his shoulders tense. "This isn't about punishment, so don't be fooled. This is about Evandria showing how powerful they are. All their members who think about stepping out of line will think twice about it after today. I'm sure this is a message to those who were following Caldwell too. They could be next."

"Evandria doesn't give a shit about its members," Ellis growled. "They're all about the power."

"Where does that leave us?" Willow asked. "What do we do now?"

It was as good a lead-in as any.

"I was going to bring that very question up after breakfast. What do you want to do now? The investigation has hit a dry spell and we're going to need to sit down and figure out our next moves if we want to continue. Do you want to continue?"

There was silence, everyone looking to the other to answer. Finally Willow spoke up.

"I can only speak for myself but I want to feel safe. We've talked a lot about whether Evandria is really out to get us. I agree that we've been mostly manipulated and they wanted us to think that we were in danger but we don't know for sure. I want to lead my life without looking over my shoulder all the time, and I don't think I can do that unless we find out who ordered Caldwell to kill our husbands. It might be the rogue faction or it might be someone else but as long as they're out there, I feel like they're a threat."

"I agree," Bailey said, nodding. "The job is only partly done. There are people in Evandria that are threatened by us. We need to find out who they are and bring them to justice. Only then will I be able to sleep soundly at night."

Peyton, her body tense and rigid, had yet to weigh in. Her two friends had expressed their wish to go on which put pressure on her to agree.

"You don't have to decide now—" Ellis began but Peyton shook her head.

"I know what I want but I also know what I'm asking of you. Just like Bailey and Willow, I want us to be free of all of this. I want to live my life in peace again without worrying about my safety or yours. But that comes with a price and it's not just me that pays it. It's you. We're a team so we decide this together."

He didn't even have to think it over. "I'm there for you no matter what."

Chase's brows raised. "I guess that means we move forward, whatever that entails."

Ellis nodded in agreement. "We need to go back to square one and review everything. Even if we have to start with Gwen's murder. Maybe we'll see something we didn't before."

Willow looked at her friends as one of the dogs jumped in her lap for a cuddle. "Does this mean we're staying here? What's the verdict on being a target?"

"I'm kind of becoming fond of this place," Peyton offered with a smile. "But I do miss Wi-Fi."

"Maybe we could stay on a few more days," Josh suggested. "Just until we figure out our next moves."

Bailey stood. "I really need to get my mail and check on my house. Am I okay to make a quick visit? Just a few hours?"

Willow nodded eagerly. "I could use a visit to my place too."

Peyton raised her hand. "Me three."

"Just be careful," Ellis warned. "Look for booby traps or anything out of place. And use the buddy system. No one goes anywhere alone."

Peyton bumped him with her elbow. "Want to be my buddy?"

Hell, yes.

PEYTON WRINKLED HER nose as she walked through her house. It had been closed up for so long she could see the dust floating in the air where the sun streamed in the windows. It was also stifling hot and she zoomed the thermostat down several degrees to get it close to comfortable while they were here. They wouldn't be staying long but already her t-shirt was beginning to stick to the skin of her back.

"It could use a good cleaning," she groaned, dumping the stack of mail on the dining room table. Her neighbor had nicely been collecting it and there was quite a mountain of junk mail. She paid her bills online so there might only be one or two things in it worth the effort of digging them out.

"It's not that bad." Ellis stuck his head in the refrigerator. "You've got some cold sodas in here. Can I have one?"

"Yes, and I'll take one too. It's ninety degrees in this house. I didn't want to waste electricity cooling the place when I wasn't here but now I'm rethinking that decision."

He handed her a can and she immediately placed the cold cylinder on her forehead, sighing in relief. "I'll drink it eventually."

Popping his open, he sat down in one of her dining room chairs. "Do you want some help with this? I can probably dig out anything addressed to 'occupant.' That should make the job a little easier."

She settled into a seat and pushed the stack so it was between them. "That would be a huge help, thank you."

It didn't take long for them to separate the mail into three piles. *Junk. Might be something. Definitely something.* The only one that could go through the two piles was herself so Ellis wandered away, exploring the house. He was doing the same thing she would if they were at his place. Checking out the books, the medicine cabinet, and the photographs.

He'd been gone a little too long though. She hadn't heard a

peep out of him for at least fifteen minutes and that worried her. Had he found something truly mortifying and was rethinking their entire relationship? Her mind whizzed through all her possessions and she couldn't think if anything that would scare him off but maybe she'd forgotten. Was he scornful of her Hootie and the Blowfish t-shirt?

"Ellis," she called, walking back into the bedroom area. "Are we playing hide and seek?"

"I'm in your spare room," he answered back. "I found your photo albums."

Wincing, she hurried to see what he was looking at. There were too many pictures of her with bad hairdos and questionable fashion choices. "Just remember that everyone has an awkward phase. Mine just lasted longer than most."

She found him on the bedroom floor, photo albums spread out in front of him.

"You were cute as a button, princess. Where were these taken?"

Sitting next to him, she peered over his shoulder. "That was my high school graduation and that's a local beach. My parents threw me a big party but it rained and we ended up sheltering under the big tent the caterer set up."

He turned the page. "And these?"

"That was the same summer. We visited a friend of my father's in New York City and then went on a cruise."

She'd taken hundreds of pictures that summer. Of the city. Of the islands they'd visited. All over the ship.

"And you took all of these? They're amazing. You have an eye for composition and color."

"You're just saying that because we're sleeping together."

The look he gave her made her giggle. Ellis was such a hard ass sometimes.

"I'd say it no matter what. These are good."

He slowly paged through the album. Most of the pictures she took didn't have people in them. She liked to photograph buildings, scenery, and beaches. He paused on one of the pages, leaning closer to the picture.

He tapped the page. "Where is this one?"

She had to think for a moment. "Cayman Islands. We went snorkeling there."

"This house in the picture... Is this where you stayed?"

It was a beautiful home with a wraparound porch and large windows. "We didn't stay there. We stayed on the ship, but we visited a couple that my father knew."

"Do you remember their names?"

Was Ellis looking to go on vacation?

"Are you testing my memory after the coma? I have to admit that I don't remember. Jensen and I played on the beach for the afternoon while the grown-ups visited. Is it important?"

He nodded. "I think it is. Did you see the name of the house?"

Ellingwood.

"Homes are often named in the Caribb–"

Ellingwood.

He was smiling now, a triumphant grin that had her heart pounding and her hands shaking. Finally, a clue. And it had been here all the time.

"Ellingwood," she repeated, her voice trembling with excitement. "That was one of the streets on that sheet of paper with the three names and addresses Alex kept hidden. It is some sort of puzzle or code."

"There must be some meaning to them," Ellis agreed. "Now to figure out what."

Staring at the photograph, she couldn't avoid the truth of what this meant. Her stomach lurched and she was glad she'd been too upset to eat breakfast this morning.

Her *father* had taken them there. Somehow he was more involved with this than she'd ever believed possible.

Chapter Twenty-Four

T HE GROUP WAS happy that Peyton and Ellis had found a clue but rightfully horrified when they realized what it meant for her. They had always assumed her father knew more than he was admitting but this evidence ratcheted up his involvement to a whole new level. Charles McMillen might be involved with the rogue faction, not just a simple member of Evandria.

Determined to make progress, everyone was spread through the house working on the two remaining street names while Ellis used his law enforcement contacts to dig up the owners of the house in the Caymans. They'd recommitted themselves to the case and that meant everyone had a job that needed to be done.

Josh was tapping away at his phone as Ellis ended the call with his friend from Homeland Security. The agent had agreed to help find the couple who had owned – or still owned – Ellingwood.

"Any luck?" Ellis asked his friend who was doing searches on the street names.

"It's like looking for a needle in a haystack," Josh mumbled.

"It could be the name of anything. A house. A park. A building. A lake. It's a roll of the dice. I have new respect for cops. Your patience with work this boring is admirable."

That drew a chuckle from Ellis. "Since when have you ever known me to be patient? I bitch about it all the time—you just don't listen anymore."

Josh grinned. "That's true. I've been tuning you out for years. Let me know if you say anything important."

"I'm about to say something now. I'm going to start dinner and you get to choose. Chicken or beef?"

"Chicken," Josh answered with no hesitation. "What are we having with it?"

"I thought I'd do an oven-fried chicken with scalloped potatoes and asparagus."

"You're going to make someone a good wife one day," Josh smirked. "Do you do windows too?"

Ellis didn't bother answering instead turning to the task at hand. He needed breadcrumbs to coat the chicken along with eggs and milk. He reached up to open the cabinet and the door almost came off in his hand. It hung sadly from the bottom hinge, barely holding on and looking like it could go at any minute. This house needed a loving dose of maintenance. The front door stuck, the garage door needed to be replaced, the microwave didn't work, the kitchen faucet was leaky, and the shower in the bathroom did as well. Nothing huge, just little things that were beginning to wear on Ellis's already brutalized nerves.

"Son of a bitch."

Josh looked up from his phone. "We can fix that. It's easy.

All I need is a screwdriver and I can put that hinge back on."

"I would have fixed it on day one if I had a screwdriver," Ellis growled. "I looked in all these drawers and the garage too. Came up with nothing."

"Did you try a butter knife?"

Ellis wasn't sure how to even answer that question. "No. Do you use a spoon to tune up your car?"

Josh laughed and put down his phone. "Seriously, you can use a butter knife in place of a screwdriver sometimes, although it scratches the hell out of them. I have a better idea. Why don't you check that shed in the backyard before we mutilate the flatware? Maybe whoever lived here kept their tools there instead of the garage."

"It's padlocked shut."

Not that Ellis cared about those things but this wasn't his house. He was trying to be respectful of Peyton and her parents.

"You're a cop. Surely you can figure out a way to get it open. Plus, what could be in there anyway that needs to be secure? A lawnmower from 1972? Pliers from the Summer of Love?"

Josh had a point. Ellis could buy a new padlock if the crown jewels were in there and needed to be protected.

"Want me to get my tire iron?" Josh asked. "We can knock the damn thing off of there."

"Rookie," Ellis taunted. "Give me five minutes and meet me out there. No tire iron needed."

It only took two minutes for Ellis to get what he needed in the kitchen – a flashlight and a paperclip – and Josh was waiting for him at the door of the shed.

"Educate me," Josh said, stepping back so Ellis could work

on the lock.

"Watch and learn." He held up the paperclip he'd straightened and broken into two pieces. Using the two thin metal rods he had the lock open in seconds.

"I'm impressed."

Ellis laughed and tucked the pieces into his pocket. "Don't be. You can learn this on YouTube. I actually learned it from another cop. Basically these padlocks are just for show. They're not the best way to secure your belongings."

"But you were avoiding opening this shed."

"Out of respect, not because I couldn't get in. This place belongs to Peyton's mother. No way do I want to go and piss her off. Not about something this stupid, anyway."

Josh gave him a lopsided grin. "Save it for something big like grandchildren and secret societies. Good plan."

Ellis didn't really have a plan to get on the friendly side of Peyton's parents. They were probably going to hate his guts and think he wasn't good enough for her. Which he wasn't. They wouldn't want her dating a cop even if he was head of detectives.

Pushing the metal sliding doors apart, the smell of dust, dirt, and metal hit his nose, instantly making him sneeze. The bright sunshine filtered in, illuminating an interior that was surprisingly large, about ten by ten. Cabinets lined two walls along with a counter at the back wall. A lone, beat-up wooden chair sat in the middle of the shed. Ellis spied a pair of pliers on the countertop out of the corner of his eye.

Tools. Excellent.

He pushed open the doors all the way to let in as much light as possible. "I think we're in luck. This must have been some sort of workshop. Where there are pliers there are probably screwdrivers too."

Now that the entire inside of the shed was exposed, Ellis hesitated to enter. He clicked on the flashlight and ran it over the room as the back of his neck began to tingle with warning.

"What's wrong?"

That was the problem. Ellis didn't know. His cop sense was screaming in his ear not to walk in but he didn't know why.

"Maybe—"

It was then he saw it. He'd been to plenty of crime scenes so it was unmistakable. It explained why his senses were warning him to get out and stay away.

He'd smelled blood. The stench could cling to wood and other materials for years, although from the looks of the puddle under the chair it hadn't been that long. The puddle was made recently.

"Listen, Josh—"

Ellis didn't need a civilian tossing his cookies at the sight of blood.

"I see it." Terse and to the point. "I'm a goddamn vet, Ellis. I know what blood looks and smells like. That's a blood pool."

"I think the next question is what is it doing here? Did the owners have a dog that was injured?"

Josh stepped forward, kneeling down next to the pool of dried blood. "It's looks like about a pint. That's more than someone would lose with a simple wound, even a head injury."

"Maybe someone lopped off a finger with a saw."

Except what would they be doing here to begin with? The house had been empty for years. Squatters? Homeless getting out of the elements? But why put a padlock on it when they were done? It didn't make sense.

Josh pointed to the other side of the chair. "Shine the light there. I think I see something."

Ellis moved the beam of light and his stomach twisted. Two teeth. Molars.

"Jesus, can a person bleed that much from losing a couple of teeth?"

Josh shook his head. "I don't think so but maybe if they're ripped out of their head. Check the pliers on the counter."

Stepping gingerly around the bloodstain, Ellis inspected the pliers and the other small tools scattered on the countertop, including one of those picks used by dentists.

"Blood," he stated. "Was this guy some kind of amateur dentist?"

"Or a sadist?" Josh finished for him. "Look at the wear marks on the chair. Someone might have been tied to it."

Ellis knelt next to Josh to take a closer look. "Good catch, my friend."

"I watch too many of those criminal investigation shows."

"It paid off this time. Keep doing it."

They both stood, Ellis sweeping the light around the room for more signs of blood. "So let me see if I have this right. From what we see here, someone was tied to this chair while someone else pulled two of his teeth out. Then maybe inflicted more wounds that could account for this volume of blood. Is that what we're saying?"

Josh nodded. "Do you think this has something to do with Peyton's father?"

Ellis hoped the hell not. That woman had been through enough to last a lifetime.

"Supposedly, according to Peyton's mother this house is a secret. Even from her husband."

Josh pointed to the floor. "Somebody knows about it, and knows that it's empty all the time. It would be a great place to do something illegal."

"Why couldn't it just be a meth lab?"

"What do we do now?" Josh asked, stepping back out into the sunshine. Ellis followed, snapping off the flashlight.

"For now, let's not touch anything. This could be something sinister or it might be innocent. A couple of vagrants and one has a toothache or some shit like that. We're paranoid as hell and I don't want us jumping to conclusions because of it."

Josh's brow quirked up. "Do you really believe that?"

"Let's just say I'm not concerned about the cabinet anymore. We've got much bigger problems. This house may not be as safe as we thought."

Chapter Twenty-Five

P EYTON COULDN'T BE shocked anymore. After everything she'd learned in the last month – things she would have never believed were true – learning someone might have been tortured in the shed didn't even rate in her top ten.

"My mother specifically said that no one knows about this place."

They were all gathered in the living room so that Josh and Ellis could fill them in on their discovery. Ellis was pushing for them to leave the house, having decided that it wasn't safe after all.

He pulled her into his embrace so her head was resting on his chest. They were sprawled on the olive green couch and Peyton could see the looks of disbelief on the faces of her friends. It had come to the point that no one knew what was true anymore.

"If it makes you feel any better she probably really believed it, but your father may have found out. It's hard to keep secrets in a marriage from what I've observed."

"The whole thing is creepy," Willow declared, shuddering.

"They pulled out someone's teeth with pliers."

"Assuming that they had nefarious purposes," Ellis replied. "There is the remote possibility that this is all quite innocent but I highly doubt it. People that break into places don't usually lock up after they leave."

Bailey's troubled gaze swept over the room. "Do you think they did things in the house too?"

Peyton had thought about that as well, which was why she wasn't anxious for dinner. Her stomach was too queasy to even think about putting food in it.

Josh rubbed the back of his neck. "It's possible. We know that the place was cleaned before Peyton and Ellis got here."

Ellis's hold on her tightened. "My vote is that we get out of here. We don't know if or when these people will come back. I may have felt safe a few hours ago but not any longer."

Josh nodded in agreement. "I'm with Ellis on this. We don't know who these people are or what they were doing here but they think this house is empty."

A quick vote was taken and it was unanimous. They were leaving. Peyton headed into the bedroom to pack the few things she had, Ellis on her heels. That determined expression he was wearing told her he had more to say but it was for her ears only.

"If you ask me if I'm okay, I'm going to scream," she warned him as he shut the bedroom door. "I feel like I've been asked that a million times in the last few weeks and I can't take it anymore."

"I don't need to ask, princess. You're not okay. Willow and Bailey aren't okay. I doubt any of us are, to be honest."

She retrieved her small bag from the closet. Packing wouldn't take more than a minute or two and she could do it for both of them.

"The universe isn't cutting us any slack." She shoved her dirty laundry into a plastic bag before packing it. Maybe she could do some wash wherever they were going.

"No, it isn't, but we just have to keep hitting back. Don't let it win."

She looked up from her packing. "Is your father possibly complicit in several homicides and who knows what else?"

Ellis sighed and shook his head. "The worst thing my old man did was root for the Yankees when we lived in Boston for a few years. I think he did it just to piss everybody off."

It was a cold day in hell when Ellis Hunter was the voice of reason in any situation.

"Then don't pretend to know how I feel. Shit, I don't even know how I feel. Right now, I'm trying not to feel anything to be truthful. My father and I have had issues my entire life but this is off the charts horrible." She had to know the truth. "Answer me, please. Do you think my father had people use this house to torture and possibly kill someone?"

Sitting heavily on the bed, Ellis slumped over, resting his elbows on his knees. "I don't know."

"Do you think it's possible?" she persisted. She wanted a goddamn answer.

"Yes, it's possible," he said hoarsely, still not looking her in the eye. "Anything is technically possible."

She shoved the rest of their clothes in the bag along with their toothbrushes. "You answered the question by avoiding it."

"Jumping to conclusions would be the worst thing we could

do. We need more information. Your father could have been an innocent pawn in all of this."

"I suppose that's true." A month ago she might even have believed it. Pushing their clothes down, she zipped up the bag. "I packed for both of us. Where are we going?"

Ellis stood and pulled her into his strong arms, his body solid as the proverbial rock. She couldn't stop herself from leaning against him, using his strength when she felt so incredibly weak. She had so many questions but no answers. The thought of doing this without him was unthinkable.

"Good question. Is there truly a safe place? I'm not sure there is. I was thinking a hotel outside of the area. Maybe Orlando or Sarasota. Then we can change up in a few days."

This was her life now. On the run. Ducking and hiding from shadows. Was she in danger? Was she not? Nobody knew the real truth.

Just how Evandria wanted her to feel.

Caressing his stubbly cheek, she lifted up on her tip-toes and pressed a kiss to his chin.

"Wherever you want to go. I trust you."

A knock on the door interrupted their kiss. To Peyton's delight, Ellis grumbled as he let in Chase, who had a smile on his face in direct contrast to his friend's grouchy mood.

"What are you so happy about?"

Chase just laughed at Ellis after giving Peyton a wink. "You really are a bear with a sore paw at times. I've a good mind not to tell you about my discovery."

"Talk."

Not perturbed in the least by his friend's growl, Chase

showed Ellis his phone. "We got a hit. An office building in Winter Park. It has the same name as one of the streets on Alex's paper."

Ellis's gloom and doom instantly turned to something far different. His eyes lit up and he stood straighter. He had a tangible goal and that made all the difference.

"Sounds like we have a field trip then."

THE NEXT MORNING, Chase and Ellis sat in their car watching the front entrance of the small office building. This was hour number three. They'd arrived early, just as the sun was coming up and inspected the outside of the building as thoroughly as possible. According to the property tax records they'd been able to dig up, this building – Herringford Centre – belonged to a company called Arsenal Architecture, Inc.

That could not be a coincidence.

Arsenal Architecture appeared to be a shell corporation, however, owned by another corporation which was owned by a third. It would take some research to untangle the spaghetti of holding companies to find out who actually owned the building. Ellis was sure that was by design.

He didn't know what they were going to find; probably nothing, but they'd mutually decided to stake out the building to see if anyone showed up or exited. So far they'd eaten a dozen donuts and drank a hell of a lot of coffee but the office building was deserted.

"We're probably wasting our time," Ellis sighed. "It doesn't look like anyone works here. We can go if you want to."

Chase's lips twisted. "I hate to fucking give up but I think you're right. Our best bet is to find out who owns this building along with that house in the Caymans. See how they're connected to Peyton's family."

"Our best bet is exactly what I'm afraid of," Ellis replied bluntly.

"How is she holding up?"

"She's the strongest woman I've ever known. She's hanging in there but she doesn't deserve this shit."

Chase nodded. "None of the women do, but I have to admit that this has been especially hard on Peyton, what with suspecting her father and maybe her brother too."

"I'm just hoping her father is like most of these Evandria members. Faithful to what they think is the mission but they don't look too deeply at their leaders." He glanced over his shoulder at the deserted block. This might just be the quietest street in America. They hadn't seen a car in at least twenty minutes. "Do you want to go?"

Chase started the engine and pulled out of the parking space in the strip mall lot across the street. They'd wanted to stay out of sight in case there was someone in the building.

"We might as well. Are we heading back to the hotel or do we have other business first?"

"The hotel. I need to call my FBI friend and see if he's found anything."

They had barely pulled out onto the street when another car came from the opposite direction and turned into the small lot in front of the office building, parking right in front of the door.

Cursing, Chase turned at the stop sign and pulled off on the side of the road where they had an excellent vantage point to watch the car and the entrance but weren't in direct line of sight.

Ellis readied his cell phone to take a picture of the driver and his license plate. "If we had left one minute earlier…"

Quickly snapping photos of the car and plate, they waited, holding their breath until the driver's side door finally opened and a man climbed out of the car. Ellis's heart rose into his throat and then fell to his stomach when he recognized who it was.

Jensen.

"That's her brother."

Ellis heard Chase's sharply indrawn breath but his friend didn't comment on the mess they were uncovering one clue at a time. Jensen and his father were in this Evandria shit up to their necks.

Jensen unlocked the office door and disappeared inside while Ellis and Chase sat in their vehicle, neither one saying a word. There would be time to talk. A few minutes later Jensen came back out, a file tucked under his arm. He climbed into his car and pulled back out onto the street.

Chase revved the engine. "Do we follow?"

"Hell, yes. I want to know where the little peckerhead is going. He and I are going to have a long talk. I'm sick of people lying to me. I warned him and he didn't listen."

Chapter Twenty-Six

PEYTON KNOCKED ON the front door of Jensen's home in Midnight Blue Beach. After hearing Ellis's story about seeing her brother at the office building and then following him to a house that had turned out to be her parents' home, she had no choice but to confront her brother. Clearly he'd been lying through his teeth in London and was far more involved than he'd let on.

Sadly, she hadn't been all that shocked when Ellis and Josh had recounted their morning. Something deep inside her had known this for a long time. Now she had proof that she wasn't crazy.

The door swung open and Jensen stood there, eyes wide with surprise. "Sis, I didn't know you were stopping by. Come on in."

"I didn't call on purpose."

She and Ellis followed Jensen into the living room, perching on the edge of the couch cushions. Jensen remained standing. It was a clear giveaway from her brother that he was nervous.

He damn well ought to be.

Ellis had agreed to take the back seat on this at the beginning so she plunged right on in.

"What business did you have at the Herringford building this morning?"

Jensen's jaw went slack. "I've never heard of the Herringford building. Is it one of our holdings?"

"Stop lying," Peyton snapped. She could feel the heat in her cheeks as her anger and frustration grew. He actually believed he could play dumb and she'd buy it and leave. "You were seen, so don't be an asshole your entire life, brother dearest. Start talking about who owns that building, what you were doing there, and what your real job in Evandria is. Don't stop until you've told me the truth. All of it."

Pacing back and forth in front of the large bay window, Jensen didn't answer right away, instead taking his time to gather his thoughts.

Or make something up. At this point, she couldn't trust him to tell the truth about the weather outside. Finally he halted, his shoulders rising and falling rapidly with his breathing.

"I don't know who owns that building. Dad asked me to go get a file there so I did."

Ellis leaned forward at the mention of her father. "Did you have keys? What file were you supposed to retrieve?"

"Dad gave me a set of keys and said that no one would be there. I assumed it was one of our office buildings. As for what file, it was on Grant Hollister."

Grant? How did he fit into all of this?

"Did you see what was in it?" Peyton asked sharply.

Jensen shook his head. "No, I didn't bother to look. I assumed it was research Dad had commissioned on Hollister. He's up for Caldwell's position as president of Evandria."

"Our father is up for president?"

Her brother laughed. "No, Hollister. He's got a real chance, too. He's very popular with the membership."

Peyton and Ellis exchanged a quick glance. This threw a whole new light on Grant. Willow was convinced he could be trusted but now Peyton had her doubts. Was he taking over for more power or was he trying to clean up the organization? She did remember what he'd said.

Trust no one. Not even her own family.

"Do you remember when we were kids and went on that cruise in the Caribbean?" Peyton asked. "We visited some friends of Dad's on the Cayman Islands. Do you know who they were?"

Frowning, Jensen chewed his lip. "I remember the vacation and I remember visiting some of Mom and Dad's friends. This was the Caymans?"

Peyton nodded and pulled the photo from her purse, handing it to her brother. "It was a beautiful house located on the beach. It was called Ellingwood."

He looked it over and shrugged. "I remember going there but I don't remember their names. Is it important?"

She was tired of his games. "Do you have so little curiosity about what our father has you do? Do you not care if he has you doing something illegal or immoral? Is that all you are? A flunky for Dad? I thought you had more original thought than that but I guess I was wrong."

Color flooded Jensen's face. "You have no idea what we're doing."

Ellis stood, his hands on his hips. "Then educate us. What

are you and your father doing in Evandria? You said you didn't know what side you were fighting on but I think that's bullshit. You should have been an actor, Jensen. You had us fooled for a little while but I'm on to you and I'm rapidly losing patience."

Smirking, Jensen clearly didn't take the warning seriously. "What is the cop going to do? Shoot me?"

It happened so fast Peyton had barely taken a single breath when Ellis had her brother by the shirt pressed up against a wall. Their faces were only a few inches apart and Jensen was now seeing what Ellis Hunter looked like when he had had enough bullshit.

It was her turn to smirk. "I could have warned you, brother dear, but I remembered that you have to learn everything the hard way."

Ellis banged him against the wall a few times. "Now, before I have to beat the living shit out of you, tell me what you and your father are doing in Evandria and the real fucking reason you're having Grant Hollister investigated."

Jensen raised his hands in surrender, darting a glance to his sister and then back to Ellis.

"Okay, I'll tell you what I know, which isn't much, I swear. In Evandria they don't encourage people to ask questions."

Backing off slightly, Ellis kept hold of Jensen's shirt. "So...talk. We're listening."

LYING IN THE king-sized hotel bed later that night, Peyton cuddled close to Ellis, her fingers absently stroking his chest.

After listening to Jensen's story and then talking it over with their friends, she was at a loss as to what to do. Her brother had insisted that he and their father were working on the side of good in Evandria, battling the rogue faction. As far as Jensen knew, Grant Hollister was honest and trustworthy, a man to lead the next generation of Evandria and work to clean up the rogue faction.

It was what he'd told them next that was the hardest to believe... Supposedly Charles McMillen had sent his only son to that office building to steal the rogue faction's file on Grant. Apparently it was going to be a deadly battle for the presidency of the organization. Winner take all. The group was on the precipice and it could tip either way, depending on how the wind blew.

"Do you believe him?" she finally asked, staring out into the darkness. A sliver of light coming through the curtains cast shadows around the room.

She couldn't see Ellis's face but she could hear the steady thump of his heart under her ear and feel the strength and comfort in his strong arms wrapped so securely around her. After everything she'd been through and learned about her own family and husband, she should have been cowering in a corner somewhere but with this man at her side she felt like she could get through anything.

That was love. She was sure of it.

"I don't know." Ellis's voice was hushed in the empty silence. "Let me put it this way. I think he believes it."

"I've had issues with my father over the years – and with my mother too but to a lesser extent – he's difficult, arrogant, condescending, and he doesn't listen worth a damn. But he's my father, and I don't want him to be an evil person. I don't want him to be a killer or someone who sanctioned it."

Her mind simply wouldn't allow her to sleep. There was too much going on and so much to think about. She'd already come to grips with the reality that she'd been blind most of her life to what was happening in her own family. Because she'd hated to even be involved in the day to day affairs of being a McMillen, she'd turned away and concentrated on anything but them. Now she could see how that had kept her from uncovering the truth, and they'd been happy to keep her in the dark. If she'd been more content with her role as Charles McMillen's daughter would she be a member of Evandria now? It was highly likely, considering her father had married her off to a member of Arsenal. He must have never lost hope that she'd return to the family fold.

Sitting up, she strained to see Ellis in the darkness. "We have to speak to him. If he's truly fighting the rogue faction, we have to know what he knows. Maybe we can help each other."

Ellis reached up and snapped on the bedside lamp, making her blink until her eyes adjusted to the light. "I think you're right but I also believe you need to temper your expectations of what he's going to share with us. So far, no one has given us a decent answer to any of our questions. All we get is obfuscation and ambiguity, and your father has given us no reason to believe talking to him will be any different. Hell, it might even be worse."

She leaned back against a pillow. "I can't argue with your logic. Maybe it's a little girl that wants to believe in her daddy, but once he sees how much we've learned in such a short time I think he might open up."

Ellis was conspicuously silent.

"Your thoughts?" she prompted when he wouldn't speak up. It wasn't like him not to give her his opinion whether she wanted it or not.

"You won't like them."

"Probably not," she sighed. "But go ahead anyway. I'm getting used to how pessimistic you are. I've decided to find it enchanting."

"If your father is high up in the organization…"

His voice trailed away and she had to nudge his arm to keep him talking.

"And?"

"What if he's not on the good side of Evandria? What if he's playing with the rogues? Doesn't that mean—well, you know?"

The thought had already crossed her mind a thousand times since she'd talked to Charles McMillen that day in London. If her father was a senior member of Evandria, and was in a leadership position in the rogue faction…

That meant her own father was trying to have her killed.

Chapter Twenty-Seven

"WHAT DID YOU tell Chase?" Peyton asked as they walked up the stone path to the front door of her parents' Midnight Blue Beach home the next morning. He wanted to get this conversation – or rather interrogation – with her father over as quickly as possible. It was doubtful that Charles McMillen was going to welcome their questions.

"I told him we'd come by as soon as we were done here," Ellis replied, straightening his tie and then giving his shoulder holster a small pat to reassure himself that his gun was still safely stowed away.

This was Peyton's family so the chances of anything danger-ous happening was low but he wasn't going to take any chances. This case had taught him two things: Trust no one and expect the unexpected. If the butler pulled a Rambo and opened fire on them, Ellis wouldn't be shocked. Or unprepared.

Peyton shifted her handbag to her shoulder. She was nervous about confronting her old man about his role in Evandria and there was not much Ellis could do to make her feel better. Considering how their last meeting went, nothing about this was going to be pleasant except the tea.

"We should all have lunch together. I know that Willow's been upset and trying to get ahold of Grant. She's worried that he's in danger now that his hat is in the ring for head of the organization."

"I kind of got the feeling that Hollister could take care of himself."

"I did too but that isn't going to stop Willow from worrying. She believes Grant is on the right side and that makes him a target."

Ellis wasn't inclined to trust anyone at this juncture.

"What do you believe?"

"I think Willow has excellent instincts about people. What about you?"

"I think I read people pretty well too." His phone buzzed in his pocket and he checked to see who was texting him. "It's my contact at the FBI. It could be important."

Peyton reached across him to ring the doorbell. "Maybe he found out something that could help us."

Ellis read the text with growing disbelief. This wasn't what he'd expected at all.

"What's your mother's maiden name?"

Peyton frowned at the question. "Patterson, why?"

"The house in the Caymans is owned by the Patterson Family Trust as is the building Jensen stole the file from yesterday."

"My mother owns Ellingwood? Then who were those people who lived there?"

There was disbelief in her tone but they didn't have a chance to discuss this new wrinkle. The door swung open and a different butler than the one from London stood there to usher them inside.

The house was decorated in the same stuffy style, way too formal for a home on the beach, but Ellis couldn't picture Peyton's parents walking barefoot in the sand so the furnishings were fitting.

The butler led them straight through the house and into an office with large windows that overlooked the Gulf of Mexico. This was the multimillion dollar view. Emerald green water met a crystal clear blue sky with the horizon dotted here and there with sleek white boats.

Charles McMillen sat at an oversized desk with his back to all that natural beauty. For Ellis, it summed up the man perfectly. He didn't see what was all around him, focusing instead on objects and money.

"I was surprised to get your call, Peyton Elizabeth."

Ellis had a feeling that the only person in the world to call her that was her father.

"We have quite a bit to discuss."

Peyton managed to keep her voice cool and controlled. Ellis was proud of how calm she appeared. This meeting was emotional but so far she'd played it low key. They'd decided that this would be the best way to approach her father. A big display of anger or indignation would likely turn him off and keep him from talking.

Her father's gaze flickered to Ellis, clearly annoyed. "Do we have company for this?"

"We do," she said firmly, linking her arm with Ellis's. "May we sit down or do you want to discuss this elsewhere?"

The old robber baron didn't even bother to stand, simply clearing his throat and motioning to the couch against the wall.

"Hampton can get you a drink."

It was nine-thirty in the morning.

"Thank you, but it's a little early for me, Mr. McMillen."

The older man's eyes narrowed. "I meant coffee or tea."

It was fun to get under her father's skin. He was way too sure of himself.

"I'll pass. Peyton?"

Her fingers gripped Ellis's arm tightly but she shook her head. "None for me, thank you."

Hampton nodded and exited the office, leaving the three of them alone. There was silence for a long moment before Peyton opened up with a question. A different one than planned in light of the text he'd received before they'd come in.

"I'd like the truth about your role in Evandria, Father. No more lying. I saw you at Archer Caldwell's trial, and I know that you had Jensen steal that file on Grant Hollister. Are you trying to get control of the organization?"

The only telltale sign of Charles McMillen's irritation at being questioned was the slight tightening of the man's jaw. He would have been a great professional poker player. But then he already was in a way as a world class businessman and financier.

"You know nothing. You only think you do."

Peyton's lips flattened into a determined line. "I know enough and most of it doesn't paint you or any of your fellow Evandrians in a positive light. I also believe that my life and the lives of my friends are in danger. People in Evandria have tried to kill me more than once. So I think I'll ask you straight out.

Do you want me dead, Father? Has what we've uncovered about Arsenal and the civil war among the members threatened you that badly? What are you willing to do for your brothers?"

Color drained from Charles's face and he pushed back from the desk as if to gain more space to breathe. "How dare you accuse me of that. You're my daughter."

"Barely," Peyton replied, her voice hushed. "I'm well aware I've been a huge disappointment to you over the years—you've made that clear enough, but do you want me dead too? Let me ask you a simpler question. Why did you want me to marry Greg? Did you know he was in Arsenal?"

McMillen was trembling now, the color back in his face and turning red. He raised his fist and brought it crashing down onto the desk with a bang. "Of course I knew. I wanted you to be safe. I did it for you."

"Peyton was in danger?" Ellis asked, his arm going around her shoulders protectively.

The older man folded his hands on the desk and stared at them for a long time, eventually standing and walking to those windows and looking outside at the bright sunshine.

"My actions may have placed my entire family in danger," he finally said, still turned away.

"Your actions?" Peyton echoed. "What actions were those?"

Her father sighed and shook his head. "What you're doing is dangerous."

Peyton sprang to her feet. "Apparently just walking around and breathing in oxygen isn't safe. I'm in danger whether I find the truth or not so you might as well tell me. What did you do that put us in this position?"

McMillen paced the small area in front of the windows. "I did it for all the right reasons."

Ellis also stood, placing himself between Peyton and her father. "I'm sure you did, sir. What exactly did you do? Are you a leader in the rogue faction?"

Her father abruptly halted and looked at Ellis as if he were crazy. "Of course not. I've fought the shadow organization with all that I am and all that I have. I've dedicated the last forty years of my life to taking them down and that's what has put my family into harm's way. They might be hurt or killed in retaliation."

Ellis wanted to believe the older man; he was Peyton's father after all, but there were still some unanswered questions.

"Did Greg know?" she asked, moving toward her father. "Is that why you wanted me to marry him? So I'd be safe?"

Sweat had broken out on Charles's forehead. "Greg didn't know my role in Evandria but I did believe that being married to a member of Arsenal would keep you safer. He was aware of threats that most members never knew existed. If there was danger, he'd make sure you stayed out of it. What I didn't count on was his weakness. The boy had a few nasty vices and he hurt you. I'm sorry about that. I never meant for that to happen."

"You pushed two people together who didn't love each other and you're surprised when it doesn't work out and turns ugly," Ellis marveled. "What did you think was going to happen?"

Her father shrugged. "Buffy and I were no great love match but we've managed to stay together all these years. Through good and bad."

Ellis didn't quite know how to respond to that but then he'd never considered tying his life to a woman he didn't love. What McMillen was talking about was empire building, not marriage.

"Speaking of Mother..." Peyton rubbed at her temple. Ellis should have made her take a pain pill before they left. She still had a tendency to get headaches when under stress like this. "How much does she know? She never wanted me to be part of the organization. Is this why?"

Shaking his head, Charles fell back into his chair. "Your mother knows almost nothing about my role in Evandria and it works well for us. She never liked the amount of time I dedicated to the group. She also knew you weren't much for our way of life, Peyton. You wanted to be free and unencumbered and you let us know often. I was quite content to let her dissuade you but I made sure you were protected. That's where Greg came in. He was the son of a family friend who I knew I could trust implicitly."

Trust no one. Charles hadn't received the memo.

"Your wife's family owned the building you sent your son to yesterday. Was that your file on Grant Hollister?" Ellis asked.

McMillen's brows pinched together. "I don't know what you're asking. I only sent Jensen to retrieve the file from the rogue faction. I didn't send him anywhere else."

Peyton perched on the arm of the sofa. "Mother owns that building."

The older man looked confused and Ellis decided to start at the beginning. "Why don't you tell me what job you gave Jensen to do yesterday."

"I sent Jensen to a building owned by one of the most senior members of the rogue faction. I'd heard they had a file on Grant

Hollister and we needed to know what they were planning to use in the election of a new leader. I sent Jensen to steal it."

"He had a key," Peyton prompted. "Where did you get it?"

"For want of a better description? A double agent. He knew that the building would be empty and where the file was located. He gave me a copy of the key and I sent Jensen there. This isn't the first mission he's done for Evandria."

Ellis's mind whirled as he took in everything they'd learned over the last several weeks plus what Charles McMillen revealed today. A picture was beginning to emerge and Ellis didn't like it at all. This was one time he'd pray to be wrong.

He took a deep breath and plunged in. "What is the name of the senior member of the rogue faction?"

The older man shook his head. "I don't know. The most senior members of Evandria are mostly a secret. They can trace their family roots back to the very beginning of the group."

Peyton's eyes squeezed closed and a noisy breath escaped her lips. "As I said, Mother owns that building. At least her family trust does."

"That's impossible."

Christ, this family was so fucked up and they had no idea. They had so many secrets from each other it might take a month of confessions to uncover them all, maybe much longer. It was a miracle Peyton had turned out as normal as she had.

Rubbing the back of his now aching neck, Ellis struggled to put into words what his brain was screaming in his ear.

What was the old saying? *There are none so blind as those who will not see.*

"It's not impossible. It's the truth. Just how much do you

know about your wife, Mr. McMillen? Or your wife's family?"

"I know everything about Buffy," McMillen said dismissively. "We practically grew up together. Our parents were best friends. What are you trying to insinuate?"

"Do you remember when we visited those friends of yours in the Caymans?" Peyton asked, her voice pleading. "Their house was called Ellingwood. Who were they? Did you know them through business?"

Charles looked puzzled. "The Caymans? Was that the cruise? Yes, I remember now." His expression cleared. "Those were relatives of your mother—distant cousins, I think. They've come to visit us here too."

Ellis had little patience with someone who had their eyes deliberately closed. Peyton's safety hinged on the truth and he was sick and tired of everyone giving him the runaround.

"Mr. McMillen, I think your wife may be involved in the rogue faction trying to take over Evandria."

It felt strange to say it out loud. It was his cop's gut talking and it rarely let him down. All the pieces were coming together now. Realizing Buffy McMillen was probably in the house and knew of their presence, Ellis rested his hand on his weapon.

Charles laughed out loud. "You must be joking–"

The man didn't get any further as the sound of a shot rang out, reverberating around the room. The piercing blast assaulted their eardrums. Instinctively, Ellis shoved a screaming Peyton into the sofa and shielded her body with his own as Charles McMillen fell into a heap, a bright red bloodstain blooming on his chest. Adrenaline spiking, Ellis whirled around and pointed his firearm at Buffy McMillen, dressed in a demure cream-colored dress, holding a pistol pointed directly at him and wearing the coldest smile he'd ever seen in his life.

She'd just shot her husband and seemed quite pleased with herself.

His heart battering against his ribs, Ellis had only one thing on his mind. Keep the woman he loved alive. He'd found the rogue faction that wanted Peyton dead.

Chapter Twenty-Eight

S HAKING WITH HORROR at what she'd witnessed, Peyton tried to run to her father's side but Ellis had an iron-grip on her waist, keeping her behind him. The image of the always formidable Charles McMillen crumpling to the floor would haunt her for years to come, of that she was sure. His expression had been so shocked as if he'd never imagined his own wife shooting him. Surely Peyton hadn't either. Her quiet, mousey mother was now wielding a handgun pointed at the chest of Ellis and clearly she wasn't afraid to pull the trigger. If Peyton wasn't terrified of Ellis being hurt or killed, she might laugh at the sheer incredulity of the situation.

"You two and your friends have become quite the thorn in my side," Buffy sighed, moving to her left to get a better look at her husband. She was so nonchalant in her demeanor that Peyton had to wonder how her father hadn't seen through her facade...or herself, for that matter. Buffy was her mother, after all. "Damn, that's an antique rug Charles is bleeding on. It will never come clean."

Peyton was too shocked to speak, her mouth dry and her

throat tight. Ellis found his voice first as his arm curled behind him and around her waist, locking her in place. At some point, he'd pulled them both to their feet but she couldn't have said when.

"Your concern for your husband's welfare is touching. Isn't shooting him a sure way to draw attention to yourself? I would think that would be the last thing you would want to do, Mrs. McMillen. You've kept a low profile all of these years on purpose and I'm guessing it has served you well."

Images of Peyton's childhood flashed before her eyes but this time with an entirely new meaning. Every moment in her mother's presence now was called into question. Buffy McMillen had fooled her daughter – and everyone else – completely. Peyton had never had a clue.

"It has." Buffy inclined her head, a serene smile on her carefully made up face. As usual, she didn't have a hair out of place. Even her Chanel suit was perfectly pressed and paired with matching pumps. "I see you've figured it out, Detective. Have you, Peyton? You're a smart girl. You're my daughter, after all."

At the mention of her name, Peyton tried to take a step forward but Ellis held her back. The arm that held a gun to Buffy's heart hadn't wavered for a moment.

"I think so. You were at Caldwell's trial, weren't you? In the other room behind the mirror."

"Yes. I knew you were there, of course, but you didn't know about me."

Ellis's arm tightened around Peyton's waist, pulling her closer. "Nigel works for you. Grant Hollister is working to take away your power."

"You are a smart one," her mother praised with a wider smile. "I should have killed you earlier but I knew Peyton had a soft spot for you. My mistake."

"You don't make many," Ellis replied confidently, his tone perfectly calm and soothing. "But letting Peyton marry Greg was one of them. He figured it all out. He and his friends knew that you were in control of the rogue faction so you had Caldwell kill them. You let Peyton live because you had a soft spot for her too."

Sweat trickled down Peyton's forehead as she surveyed her mother. A woman she'd thought she knew well but it had all been an elaborate ruse. They'd never been a happy family but this was beyond her imagination. All these years she'd resented her father but it had been her mother that was evil.

Still holding out a thread of hope, she covertly glanced at her father's chest to see if he was still breathing, but he was gray and still. Hadn't he been tough and indomitable all of her life? She could only pray that this was one of those times.

"Sadly even I am only human. The marriage was something Chuck insisted on and I couldn't tip my hand by protesting too much." Buffy waved the gun at her husband on the floor. "At first I thought Greg was just a hard partying womanizer but he was serious about his role in Arsenal. He dug up the truth about my family being one of the founders of Evandria. Apparently he had insomnia one night when the two of you were visiting, Peyton. He explored the library and found some diaries of my ancestors. It took him years of visits to get enough information but he and his friends finally did it. Unfortunately for him, he foolishly didn't cover his tracks. Nigel found out what he was investigating. That was the end of Greg and the others."

So much was crystal clear now. "That's why he insisted on staying here at the house when we visited instead of buying a place locally. The last few years he wanted to come here several times. I didn't understand. I thought he and Daddy wanted to play golf."

"They were worried about your welfare, my darling."

Peyton had always believed there was good inside of Greg and there it was. He was trying to protect her and Evandria. He'd given his life to do it. If only he'd trusted her with the truth, she could have helped him.

"Nigel," Ellis pressed. "Did he turn against you? He was the one that manipulated us into finding out about Archer."

The woman half-nodded, but Peyton could see the anger simmering under the surface. Whatever Nigel Holmwood had done, her mother was furious about it.

"He went off script. He decided he wanted more power and control. I certainly wasn't going to let that happen. But if you're asking if he pulled a few strings to send you in a certain direction, the answer is yes."

They'd joked about the universe bringing them together. Peyton wanted the truth.

"Was it Nigel who made sure all three of us were invited to that fundraiser where we met?"

Buffy's lips flattened. "That was an unfortunate accident that has caused me a great deal of trouble and effort to keep you otherwise occupied. But you should thank me, my child. I was the one that made sure the road was blocked that night so you couldn't get to Roy's on time. I wanted Hollister dead but I only wanted you to be afraid. I wanted you to be worried about someone trying to kill you so your little group didn't have time to figure out what was truly going on."

So they had been manipulated at every turn.

Funny, Peyton didn't feel so grateful at the moment.

"What about you?" Ellis challenged. "Did you ever worry about your children?"

Peyton wasn't sure she wanted to hear the answer to that question but there was no escaping from this room. Buffy McMillen raised her chin, her blue eyes an icy gray.

"I never wanted to marry or have children, Detective. I did it out of duty to my family legacy. Charles McMillen was chosen very carefully by my father. My mission in being his wife was clear. All these years I've kept my husband's efforts in check by reporting on his actions to my Evandria brothers and sisters. But I did care about my children. My dream was for them to follow in my footsteps and work for the glory of the organization but it became clear that Jensen was his father's son and Peyton didn't have the guts to do what needed to be done. She's not the type to die for a cause—or kill for it either."

It didn't even hurt. Hearing her mother say Peyton was weak didn't even begin to cause any pain. She'd divorced her emotions from her difficult parents years ago. That realization was quite freeing.

"That's where you're wrong, Mother," Peyton said, her tone sharp. "I'm not weak. I'm stronger than you could ever imagine. Did you have me blown up too? You must have been disappointed when I lived. Sorry about that."

"It was merely meant as a warning," Buffy replied, a serene

expression on her face. "I'm just sad that you didn't take it. As for your strength, you have surprised me. But you still don't have what it takes. Life is messy, my dear, and sometimes the things you have to do are too."

Peyton's stomach lurched when she remembered the scene in the shed at the house. "The house you lent us. The one that was supposed to be so safe. You killed someone there, didn't you?"

Buffy shook her head. "Not me, but some of my associates. We use that property to...interrogate those we need information from. Actually I own most of the property in that area and all the residents work for me. However I had no idea the people who worked for me had been so sloppy. How did you know?"

Ellis took one step back, pulling Peyton along with him. "Blood and teeth. You need to tell your goons to clean up after themselves a little better. If you didn't want us to find that, why did you send us there?"

"So I would know where you were. It made keeping an eye on you so much easier. You kept finding the cameras and listening devices so I simply put you in the center of my employees."

Peyton snuck another look at her father. If he wasn't already gone, he needed help right away. They needed to bring this to an end, but how? Ellis and Buffy each had a weapon and neither were going to give it up easily. Maybe the servants had heard the shot?

"You killed my husband and my friends' husbands."

"They were lousy men. The world is better for their deaths."

"You don't get to decide that, Mother."

Buffy McMillen sidled over to the desk, the firearm still

trained on Ellis and Peyton. "That's where you're wrong. I'm going to do it again. Right now, as a matter of fact. I've decided you both have to die. I know you don't see it this way, Peyton, but it's an honor to die really. Gwen was sacrificed for Evandria's glory. Her parents understood that we must do whatever is necessary for the mission, even lose a child. I understand that too and I'm willing to do what needs to be done. That's the difference between you and me."

Ellis's grip on Peyton tightened to the point where she could hardly take a breath. This close, she could feel the blood pumping through his veins in time to her own racing heart. Did he have a plan to get them out of this?

"What about Hampton?" Ellis asked. "Or the rest of the staff? They had to have heard the shot and now you want to fire off a few more rounds? That's bound to get more attention than you want."

The older woman shook her head. "They're too well-trained to call anyone. Besides, this room is soundproof. Chuck was paranoid about people overhearing his business conversations. His foresight was one of his better qualities."

The dark red pool around Peyton's father had grown. There was no way he could survive losing that amount of blood. Tears stung the backs of her eyes and she blinked hard to stem the tide. Now was not the time to fall apart. If they survived this, she might have a chance later.

"If you shoot me, I'll shoot you," Ellis countered, a hard edge to his voice. "Trust me when I say I have no issues pulling this trigger."

Buffy leaned against the edge of the desk, looking unruffled by Ellis's declaration.

"I believe you. That's why we're going to do this a different way. A murder-suicide. You're going to shoot Peyton and then shoot yourself."

Ellis's entire body tensed and Peyton could swear he wasn't breathing. The material of his shirt was damp under her palms from the sweat pouring down his back and neck. She wanted to say something to Ellis like how much she loved him and that she was glad she'd fallen for him even if they didn't live through this. He was the best man she'd ever known. All of a sudden she had so much to tell him – so many things she wanted them to experience together – and there didn't appear to be any more time to do it.

"Why would I do that?"

"You're going to die either way today. Now you can shoot Peyton and give her a clean and quick death or I can do it and you can watch her die slowly, bleeding to death. I'm told that's a painful way to go. It's up to you. If you love her, you should be kind."

Ellis didn't move a millimeter, firmly parked in front of Peyton. Tension radiated from his motionless frame and she tried to keep as still as possible behind him, not wanting to throw off his concentration when a gun was pointed at his heart.

"You have to shoot through me to get to her."

"Fine. I'm tired of all of this. I'll think of a good story later."

It happened in a blur of motion.

Buffy straightened from where she'd been lounging against the large oak desk, a loud explosion and a flash of light coming from the muzzle of her firearm. Ellis grunted and hunched over, his legs giving out as he sunk to the carpet, too heavy for Peyton to hold up. The firearm in his hand dropped to the floor next to him and Peyton didn't hesitate, dropping to her knees at his side and reflexively reaching for it.

This was all her fault. If Ellis was dead, it was because of her. But he'd helped her change more than he would ever know, and she wasn't the quiet little wife anymore who looked the other way because it was easier. Ellis had said she was fierce and she would show him that he was right.

Tears streaming down her face and barely able to see through them, Peyton raised the gun toward the woman she'd called Mother for thirty-five years – a woman who had shot two men in cold blood – and squeezed the trigger, the kickback sending her sprawling on her ass. Buffy McMillen's silk Chanel suit had a circle of red on the front near her abdomen and she too had fallen to the floor.

The door to the office flew open and Grant Hollister along with two other men stormed in, guns blazing. The took one look at the carnage and holstered their weapons, one of the men pulling out his phone instead to make a call.

Grant fell to his knees next to Peyton, whose fingers were still clutching the weapon, ears ringing from the gunfire. Her teeth were chattering and her body shivering as a blast of cold came over her.

"Peyton, are you okay? Are you hurt?" Hollister's gaze raked her head to toe. "We've been watching Nigel and Buffy for a long time and when Willow told me you and Ellis were here..."

"911 for Ellis," she choked out as she dropped the gun and leaned over to check her lover's pulse. Her fingers found the spot on his neck and she cried even harder, her body wracked with sobs as she felt it under her fingertips.

Ellis was alive.

Chapter Twenty-Nine

ELLIS FELT LIKE he'd been hit by a cannonball. In all the years he'd been a cop he'd never been shot, although he'd come close a time or two. A few weeks with Peyton and he took one in the abdomen, losing his spleen and gaining some bragging rights among his fellow police officers.

Thank God Buffy McMillen was a lousy shot.

The society matron might be morally fine with taking a life but apparently she didn't have that much practical experience doing it. If she'd aimed three or four inches higher he'd be dead.

Or maybe not. He wasn't leaving Peyton of his own free will. They had a life together and he wasn't going to give that up.

Waking up from anesthesia wasn't a walk in the park. It was goddamn painful, in fact. The smell of antiseptic assailed his nostrils and his thinking was muddled. His lips and mouth felt as dry as a desert. He tried to move his arm but it was connected to several tubes and he only succeeded in hurting himself as a sharp jolt shot up through his rib cage and down his left leg.

Note to self. Don't move.

"Peyton," he croaked, his fingers landing on her head where

it was lying on the bed next to him, her hair silky to the touch. Upon hearing his voice she jerked awake, blinking away the sleep and rubbing her eyes.

"You're awake," she said, relief etched in her beautiful face. "You've been asleep for several hours."

He'd been conscious when Grant had brought him to this private hospital, in and out until they'd taken him back for surgery. At least he thought it was Hollister. Had it all been a dream brought on by painkillers?

"Your parents…Hollister."

The doctors had said something about a collapsed lung and fuck, it hurt to talk or breathe. He wasn't sure if his chest hurt because he'd been shot or because his heart was simply too full of love for this woman. His warrior.

"Easy," Peyton said, smoothing his hair off of his forehead, her fingers cool against his cheek. She was a blaze of color in the drab green of the room but then she was gorgeous every moment of the day.

Who was he kidding? She was everything.

He opened his mouth but she shook her head and pressed her hand to his lips.

"If you promise not to talk too much, I'll explain what's happened in the last twelve hours. Promise? Then I need to let them know you're awake."

He nodded but it wouldn't be easy. Silence wasn't his natural state.

His gaze ran around the room. Private, which his insurance sure as hell didn't cover. The bed was pretty comfortable for a hospital too, along with the pillow and blanket. There was even a big screen television on the wall. All that was missing was a wet bar.

"First off, we're in a Midnight Blue Beach clinic I didn't even know existed. It's for Evandria members exclusively. Whenever I drove by here I thought it was a nursing home for the elderly. Grant said you had the best surgeon in the United States."

Knowing these Evandria types, Ellis believed it.

A sob escaped and her shoulders shook. "I know we joked about you taking a bullet for me but you didn't have to actually do it, you idiot."

If Ellis's recollections of the scene were correct, her mother had been hell bent on killing both of them. The fact that only one of them had been shot was a miracle he wasn't going to question.

She glanced over her shoulder at the closed door. "Grant brought you and my parents here. His friends helped."

Ellis had a vague recollection of two men with Grant but their faces were fuzzy.

Coughing, Ellis struggled to get out the words. "Did they...?"

She shook her head, tears rolling down her already red cheeks. Her eyes were swollen and he had a feeling she'd been crying for some time. He wanted to make everything better but this was one hurt he couldn't fix.

She pointed toward the door. "Dad didn't make it and neither did my mother. I mean Buffy. Jensen is out there working with Grant to create a cover story for all of this and to plan the funerals. They're leaning toward saying they were in a car accident."

"Nigel?"

"He's been taken into custody. Evandria custody."

After seeing Caldwell's fate, they all knew what that meant. Bailey was going to be devastated.

Stroking his hand, she gave him a brave smile. "Evandria had an emergency meeting and installed Grant as president, along with his two friends as his chief of staff and vice president. He's in control and already has many of the rogue faction in custody." A sob choked her and she had to take several deep breaths before she could continue. "We did it. We brought them down."

So drugged up he could barely respond, he had to make due with squeezing her hand as a lump grew in his own throat. There had been so many times he'd never thought they'd see this day come but it had.

At such a terrible price. His girl had lost so much.

A tear fell onto the back of his hand and she sniffled, grabbing a tissue from the side table.

"Greg, Frank, and Alex are being hailed as heroes. You too. Grant offered us lifetime membership." She pressed a hand to her cheek. "I said we'd have to think about it."

A member of Evandria. That would be...surprising...but he did respect Hollister and what the man was trying to do.

He sucked in a painful breath to get the next words out. "Chase...Josh..."

She nodded, scrubbing at her tears. "They're in the waiting room along with Willow and Bailey. They can't wait to see you but the doctors would only let me stay in here. Is there anything I can get you? Do you want some water?"

Water sounded like the most wonderful thing in the world. He couldn't believe how thirsty he was despite what was probably a saline drip going directly into his vein.

But first...

Slowly and carefully, he lifted his unattached arm and beckoned her closer so he could whisper into her ear. She bent down, keeping to his side so she didn't press her weight onto his wound.

"What is it, Ellis? I need to let the nurse know you're awake."

The way the monitors were going crazy he was sure they knew. But he was so fucking proud of her and he had to let her know before everyone else joined them. She'd been through hell and she was going to survive it. He'd be there to help her even if it took a lifetime.

"You–"

Pain clutched at his chest and he couldn't get the words out. He had to wait and take a few breaths before trying again but she was already shaking her head.

"It's okay. You can tell me later."

He could wait but he didn't want to. This was important.

"You...are...fierce...and...I...love...you."

Her smile was the warmest sunshine on a gray day and at that moment she gifted it to him even as more tears fell.

Drawing a shaky breath, she nodded in agreement.

"I am fierce, and I love you too."

Chapter Thirty

Ten months later...

EXHAUSTED AND SORE, Peyton's heart had never been more full of love and gratitude. The universe must have been sorry about what it had done to her last year because it was doing its best to make up for it. She had never been happier or more satisfied with her life.

After all that had happened, Ellis had devoted himself to her and never looked back. They'd married six months later. There hadn't been any reason to wait, plus she was already pregnant.

Was there anything sexier than a man holding a baby?

Her handsome husband strutted around the hospital room – the same one he'd recovered in only a year ago – but this occasion was much different. This time he was showing off their newborn, daughter Sienna Marie Hunter, just six pounds, three ounces. She had Peyton's blue eyes and Ellis's dark hair. Thankfully, she also had inherited her mother's temperament, sweet and calm.

With a pout Bailey held out her arms. "It's my turn to hold her."

Ellis leaned down and rubbed his nose against little Sienna's. "Actually I think it's Willow's turn."

The blonde's eyes went wide and she held up her hands in surrender. "I think I'll stick with dogs. What if I drop her?"

"You won't drop her." Peyton giggled at the terrified look on her friend's face. "Go ahead. It'll be fine."

Reluctantly Willow accepted the sleeping child from Ellis, her features softening as she gazed down at Sienna. "She is cute."

She was beautiful, everything she and Ellis had dreamed about.

Josh leaned in and ran a gentle finger over the baby's furled fist. "Ellis said he's going to want a boy next, Peyton. Has he mentioned that yet?"

Frequently. But then she was completely on board with the idea.

"He has but I think we might wait a year or two."

Chase chuckled. "He might have to get shot again. Isn't that how this happened in the first place?"

Ellis shrug but Peyton could see his cheeks had turned a ruddy shade. "So I got bored during my recovery. The doctors wouldn't let me go back to work for months."

"No one is getting shot again," Peyton stated firmly, reaching for her husband's hand and feeling that familiar zing when they touched.

Ellis was looking at her with such love and adoration she thought her heart might explode in her chest. When she'd met him she had no idea that this man would be her destiny but she wouldn't have it any other way. They were building a life and a family together.

Something she'd never had before.

A quiet knock pulled her attention away from the man she loved. The door opened slightly and Grant stuck his head in, a grin on his face. "Is it safe to come in?"

She smiled and beckoned him inside. "Sienna wants to meet her honorary uncle."

Willow swiveled in her chair so Grant could see the baby. "I think it's your turn to hold her too."

Grant didn't appear to have one ounce of trepidation about handling the precious bundle. Placing her on the shoulder of his expensive Italian suit, he patted her back and cooed softly as if he'd been holding and caring for newborns his entire life.

"You look pretty comfortable with her," Bailey laughed. "Who knew millionaires also made great nannies."

Grant's brows shot up. "I've got mad skills in the baby department. Lots of cousins and they were all criers." He paused next to Ellis. "Listen, take all the time you need, and I'm serious about that. This is a hell of a lot more important than anything going on in the office. Finn and Silas can handle anything that comes up."

Finn and Silas were the two friends Grant had brought to the house that day ten months ago. The three men were like brothers and had managed to clean out most, if not all, of the rogue faction in Evandria but they never forgot to give credit where it was due. So much of what they'd been able to accomplish was a direct result of the efforts of Peyton and her friends.

Grant wanted a new kind of organization that wasn't committed so much to power as service. The first thing the new president had done was lift the veil of secrecy in the group.

Everyone was invited into The Clubhouse and the meetings were now open and even streamed online. Evil couldn't hide in the bright light of day.

He'd also given Nigel a reprieve from the death sentence that surely awaited him. After the trial, Holmwood had been taken to a secure location where he would live out the rest of his days under prison conditions. Grant wanted to know everything Nigel knew about the rogue faction and its history.

After his recovery, Ellis had intended to return to his post as head detective back in Virginia and Peyton had even put her house on the market. Grant, however, made them an offer they couldn't refuse. Ellis was put in charge of a revamped Arsenal now simply titled Evandria Security. He directed everything from cyber-security to new member background checks.

"That's sweet, Grant," Peyton said, accepting his kiss on her cheek. "Thank Finn and Silas too."

"I will," Grant agreed easily, his gaze on Sienna. "They wanted to be here but they both had business out of town. I do think they sent a few gifts to your home. I know I did."

"I'm well aware," Peyton groaned. "Jensen said that he's getting a delivery about every five minutes. At this rate, we're going to need a bigger house."

Peyton might have inherited half of her family's estate but she still didn't want to live the privileged lifestyle. She and Ellis had a simple home in a good school district. Jensen, having been dumped by Amelia and now back in the States, was happy to manage most of the business although she kept an eye on things.

She'd managed to grow closer to her brother as they attended therapy together to deal with their painful family secrets and past. It had been Ellis's idea and she'd been reluctant at first to tell her thoughts to a stranger but he'd been insistent that he couldn't help her heal all alone.

Grant reluctantly relinquished Sienna to Bailey, who positively glowed when she held the baby. Peyton had a feeling that a child was in Chase and Bailey's future and hopefully soon. It would be wonderful for the kids to grow up together. The couple had purchased a house not far from Peyton and Ellis.

The only thing that would make it even better? Josh and Willow close by.

"Josh, when will the sale of your practice be final?" Peyton asked. She was anxious to have all three of them together again. They had already talked about going back to that dive bar where they'd drank tequila shots that first night.

"End of the month," he replied with a smile, his arm around Willow. "But the house won't be finished for at least two."

Willow had sold all of Alex's car collection and bulldozed the warehouse. They were building a state of the art veterinary clinic, home, and animal rescue on the property instead.

Groaning, Willow rolled her eyes. "It's a full time job outfitting the house and the business. When we're done I'm going to sleep for a week."

Josh snorted. "As if the dogs will let you."

Peyton gave Ellis a meaningful look, one she hoped he'd understand. They'd talked about this when she'd gone into labor. At first he frowned but then his expression cleared and he smiled. He remembered.

"Hey guys," he said, slapping Chase on the back. "Why don't we give the women a moment?"

Josh's brow wrinkled. "Why– Oh yeah. A minute. Got it."

The men trailed out of the room, Ellis giving her a wink before he closed the door behind him. Willow and Bailey sat on the edge of Peyton's bed, one on each side, and Peyton took her daughter into her waiting arms. The warm, squirming bundle was a heavenly weight against her chest. She pressed a kiss to Sienna's forehead and vowed silently to be the best mother she could. This generation of the family would be different.

"I wanted to say something to you today." Her throat tightening with emotion, Peyton had to pause for a moment. "I just wanted to say that meeting you both was the best thing that has ever happened to me. I was just going through the motions and now I have the most wonderful life I could ever imagine. You are the best friends anyone could ask for and I am so lucky that we ran into each other that night at the party."

Willow's brow quirked. "Are you sure about that? We almost got you killed."

"We did get you drunk," Bailey reminded her. "And we found out your late husband had another family. Those aren't things you usually thank someone for."

"Painful as hell," Willow grimaced but it turned into a smile. "But I think you're right. We're a team, the three of us. We faced what the universe threw at us and survived."

"The truth set me free." Peyton shook her head as her fingers, feather light, traced her daughter's petal soft cheek. "It set all of us free."

No more secrets. No more danger.

Peyton had found the people she could trust. These friends. Her man.

A gift greater than any money or power. Friendship and love.

Thank you for reading
Midnight Blue Beach –
Kiss Midnight Goodbye

Sign up to be notified of Olivia's new releases:

oliviajaymesoptin.instapage.com

About the Author

Olivia Jaymes is a wife, mother, lover of sexy romance, and caffeine addict. She lives with her husband and son in central Florida and spends her days with handsome alpha males and spunky heroines.

Look for Olivia's new Contemporary Romance series *The Hollywood Showmance Chronicles* in the spring of 2017.

Visit Olivia Jaymes at
www.OliviaJaymes.com

Danger Incorporated

Damsel In Danger

Hiding From Danger

Discarded Heart Novella

Indecent Danger

Embracing Danger

Danger In The Night

Cowboy Justice Association

Cowboy Command

Justice Healed

Cowboy Truth

Cowboy Famous

Cowboy Cool

Imperfect Justice

The Deputies

Justice Inked

Justice Reborn

Military Moguls

Champagne and Bullets

Diamonds and Revolvers

Caviar and Covert Ops

Emeralds, Rubies, and Camouflage